Wild Pitch

Books by Matt Christopher

Wild Pitch

E. S. E. A.
Title IV B

MATT CHRISTOPHER

Little, Brown and Company
BOSTON   TORONTO

FIRST EDITION

Library of Congress Cataloging in Publication Data

Christopher, Matthew F
  Wild pitch.

  SUMMARY: Eddie doesn't like the idea of girls
playing baseball in his league, but when one of his
pitches injures a girl, he rethinks his attitudes.
  [1. Baseball — Fiction] I. Title.
PZ7.C458Wh   [Fic]   80–16060
ISBN 0–316–14019–8

BP

*Published simultaneously in Canada
by Little, Brown & Company (Canada) Limited*

PRINTED IN THE UNITED STATES OF AMERICA

To my sons,
Marty, Dale, and Duane

Wild Pitch

1

No one on the Lancers' bench, including Eddie Rhodes, paid much attention to Puffy Garfield during the first inning when he said that the Surfs had a kid by the name of Phil Monahan playing first base for them.

So the kid was a snappy first baseman. Big deal! There were a lot of snappy first basemen. Whatever else Puffy had to say about this Phil Monahan didn't impress Eddie enough for him to bother listening any further.

At the top of the fifth inning, as Eddie was grabbing his bat from the bunch standing in the metal rack, he heard Phil Monahan's name mentioned again. He looked up to see who was bringing it up this time, and saw that it was Paul Norcross. Paul was sitting next to Tip McDonald, the Lancers' husky catcher, and Tip looked as if the name meant something to him.

Eddie waited a couple of seconds to see if he could

hear any more about this Phil kid, but Coach Inger's voice cut into his thoughts.

"Get on, Eddie. Let's turn this ball game around." The Lancers were trailing the Cobras by two runs, 4–2.

"He's got a long handle on it, Eddie," said Puffy, who was short and squatty and had arms like overstuffed sausages. "Just grab it and heave it."

"I'll do that," said Eddie, grinning.

He moseyed up to the plate in his easygoing stride, took two cuts at the ball, then let four straight ones, all inches away from the plate, go by.

"Take your base!" said the ump.

Eddie turned and winked at Puffy.

"Cheap," Puffy snorted.

Eddie tossed the bat toward a small kid in a baseball uniform, who darted after it, picked it up, and dropped it into the rack. Eddie trotted to first base.

Eddie stayed on first until he got the bunt sign from Coach Inger at third. Touching the tip of his blue cap to show he understood the sign, he stepped off the bag and took a lead.

For just a few seconds his mind drifted to the name Phil Monahan again, and he wondered what could be so significant about a kid's playing first base that he would be mentioned twice within five innings. What was special about the guy? Was he a seven-foot giant, or what?

Well, he'd find out soon enough, he figured.

He saw Larry lay the bunt down to third, and Eddie bolted to second. The Cobras' third baseman made a play on it and threw Larry out. Eddie, safe at second, was now where he was planned to be — in scoring position.

He took his lead again, keeping his eye on the shortstop, the second baseman, and the pitcher. Rod Bellow came through with a double to the left-field fence. Eddie ran to third, then made a dash for home.

"Hit it!" Dale Strong yelled as Eddie came pounding toward the plate.

He wasn't crazy about sliding. He seldom slid. He liked pitching better than fielding or hitting or running. But if sliding into a base meant scoring a run, he'd just have to slide.

He hit the dirt, and dust swirled and curled up around him like smoke.

"Safe!" yelled the ump.

A cheer boomed from the Lancers' fans. There were about eighty people in the grandstand and bleachers, half of whom cheered for the Lancers.

Eddie got up and brushed himself off as he headed for the dugout.

"Nice slide, Pitch!" Tip said to him, white, gap teeth showing in a wide grin.

"Of course," said Eddie immodestly.

He and Tip had been friends since the day Eddie had moved to Argus, a small town on the southwest coast of Florida. Eddie's parents had purchased a gift shop at Bahia Vista Plaza, after having sold their home in Ohio. Tip was a native Floridian, and his father was a cop.

Puffy, sitting near the end of the dugout, leaned toward Tip and said, "Hey, Tip, you going to tell him?"

"Tell him what? Oh, yeah," Tip said.

He beamed, and a mischievous look came into his eyes.

"Shove over," Eddie said.

Tip and Tony Netro moved to give him room. He sat down and looked at Tip.

"Tell me what?" he asked.

"You know Phyl Monahan?"

Eddie frowned. "No. All I heard was that he's a first baseman. What's so hot about him?"

"It's not a him. It's a her. Her name's Phyllis. They call her Phyl."

Eddie's jaw slacked. "Huh?"

Tip chuckled. "You heard me."

6

"A girl? And she plays first base?"

Tip nodded. "And from what Puffy says, she's good."

Maybe she's good on a girls' team, Eddie reflected. But on a boys' team? He doubted it. Not that he had anything against girls. He knew some who were pretty nice. But as a ballplayer? No way. He really didn't think they belonged on the same diamond with the guys.

Eddie looked over at Puffy and caught his eye. "You know her?"

Puffy pushed out his lower lip and shook his head. "No. She lives in the Parkdale school district. That's where most of the kids go to school who play with the Surfs."

"She big?"

"You mean is she tall? No. I'd say about average."

Tip squeezed Eddie's knee. "The Surfs are playing on Number Two field. What do you say we hightail it over there after our game? If they're still playing we can get a look at her."

Eddie shrugged. Why should he go over there and watch her play? Seeing ballplayers there from another team might just swell her head, anyway. Being on a boys' team might have already swollen it a size or two.

"I don't know," he said, reluctant.

"Why not?" Tip winked. "Maybe she's got something else besides legs."

Puffy Garfield laughed. "Yeah."

They turned their attention back to the ball game, and watched Dale pop out to the shortstop. Rod ran off second a few steps, but got back before the shortstop could make a play on him.

"Knock 'im in, Lynn!" Puffy yelled to the next batter, Lynn Pellman. "You're hittin', man!"

Lynn was the Lancers' cleanup hitter. So far he had singled and grounded out. Pitchers had heard of his reputation as a long-ball hitter and tried never to give him a good pitch.

Tom Hayes didn't give him one, and Lynn dropped his bat and trotted to first.

Paul Norcross took two cuts, then struck out, leaving the two men stranded.

Tip buckled up his knee guards. "Let's hurry out there and get this game over with," he said.

"This is just the middle of the fifth inning, Tip," reminded Eddie, getting up. "And we need more runs to take this game."

"Come on, guys," said the plate umpire. "Hustle."

The teams exchanged sides, Eddie going to the mound to start pitching the bottom half of the inning. After the first inning he'd been doing fairly well. He had a strong arm, a curve, and a slowball that worked now and then. His father had taught him how to throw it. It wasn't an easy pitch. He was able to throw it so it would hardly turn, but controlling it was something else. He had a reputation for being wild, anyway. He had a good day if he didn't dust off at least two batters during a seven-inning ball game.

He got by the first Cobra batter (a pop-up to first), struck out the second, then caught a high bouncer to throw out the third batter himself.

Tip, Tony, and Puffy made it a quick one-two-three in the top of the sixth, and Eddie held the Cobras scoreless when they came to bat.

He led off in the final inning, hoping he could do something memorable for a change. So far he hadn't done enough to create even a ripple of excitement.

He did now, lambasting a triple off the left-field fence.

Standing and waiting for one of the next batters to knock him in, he got to thinking about Phyl Monahan again. He had to admit that if she was playing with the Surfs she must be good. Maybe he'd be pitching to her one of these days.

He watched Larry pop out to short. Then he scored on Rod's long sacrifice fly to deep center field.

"Nice sock, guy," said Tip as Eddie trotted in to the bench and sat down, breathing a little heavily.

"About time," Eddie said. He'd been due.

The Lancers now ripped the game wide open as Dale came through with a double, followed by Lynn's walk and Paul's second triple of the game. Tip flied out to left for the third out, and the Lancers led, 6–4.

"Let's hold 'em, men!" Coach Inger yelled as they took the field the last half of the inning.

Eddie threw in warmup pitches, faced the first batter, and dusted him off. He didn't do it intentionally, but the jeers from the Cobras' fans made him wonder if they thought he might have.

He finally walked the guy.

The next batter hit into a double play, and the next flied out to left, ending the ball game.

Eddie saw Tip throw off his mask and his belly guard, and start rapidly on his shin guards.

"Still going over to watch the Surfs?" he asked.

"Sure!"

"Okay!"

He tossed the equipment over to where the mascot was piling bats into a bag. Then he straightened his cap, picked up his mitt, and headed for the gate.

"Let's go."

Eddie saw Puffy waiting for them. In a few seconds all three were walking briskly off the diamond to field Number Two.

2

Doss Park was a huge complex of three baseball fields located about a half a mile away from the city of Argus. Each field was equipped with lights for night games, and had a grandstand and bleachers that would seat a thousand spectators.

So far the seats had never been filled to capacity, so when the boys walked in through the gate of Number Two field and saw the packed stands, they thought they were seeing a record crowd.

"Look at that," said Puffy, surprised. "It's jam-packed."

"She must be the draw," said Tip.

"She's probably getting a big charge out of it," said Eddie. "Like a movie star."

They found a place to stand next to the third-base bleachers. Eddie looked at the scoreboard and saw that it was the sixth inning. The Surfs were playing Tanglewood and had first bats. They were leading, 8–5.

11

"Who's batting?" Puffy wanted to know.

"The Surfs," Tip observed.

"You see her?" Eddie asked.

"I don't know what she looks like," answered Puffy.

Eddie started to look over the players sitting in the dugout behind first base. They all had their uniforms and caps on, and looked pretty much alike. Some had long hair, some short.

"Come on, Lee! Blast it!" yelled a fan.

The batter was a tall kid with hair down to his collar. He took a wild cut at the ball, and, from the umpire's cry, they knew he'd struck out. Head down in disgust, still holding his bat, he retreated to the bench.

"I know how you feel, kid," said Puffy sympathetically.

The next batter walked up to the left side of the plate, tapped it twice, then got ready for the pitch.

"This Phyl Monahan," said Eddie. "She bat left or right?"

Puffy shrugged his shoulders. "I don't know. I told you I've never seen her."

"Send it out of the lot, Mike!" cried a fan.

Tip smiled. "Well, we know *that's* not her," he said.

Eddie forgot his adverse feelings about a girl

playing on a boys' baseball team, and he smiled, too. Mike, wobbling to the plate, was big and round, and the back of his shirt was stained with sweat. "Catcher" was written all over him.

He laced out a fly to center, and was only halfway to first base when it was caught.

The Tanglewoods came in; the Surfs went out. Eddie watched to see which player would be heading toward first base.

"There she is," Tip said.

Then Eddie saw her, too. She was holding her mitt in her hand, folded over. Two long, blond pigtails stuck out from underneath her red baseball cap and bounced on the back of her neck as she trotted out to her position at first base.

"She could pass for a boy if it weren't for those pigtails," said Tip.

"Yeah," said Eddie.

He hoped that a ball would be hit to her. He was anxious to see how she'd handle it. Playing first base was no picnic.

He watched her field the grounders that the infielders threw over to her and had to admit she looked good at it. She was right-handed. She squatted down with both hands, scooped up the ball, straightened up, and threw to the next fielder with grace and ease.

13

Well, you couldn't judge a player's ability much by these warmup throws, Eddie told himself. It was how you performed in a game that counted.

Tanglewood's first batter drove a long fly to deep center field for a double. The next guy bashed one to the shortstop, who faked the runner back to second, then pegged to first to get the hitter by two steps. Phyl Monahan stretched to make the catch, then quickly got off the bag and got set to throw to third when the runner on second made a motion to run there. He stopped, and she tossed the ball in to the pitcher.

"Well, what do you think?" asked Puffy.

"Think?" echoed Eddie, frowning. "She hasn't done much. All she's done is catch a ball."

"Right," agreed Tip. "My little sister can do just as well."

She had another putout during the half inning, and then a chance at a high-bouncing one-hopper. She leaped, grabbed it, came down on both feet, stepped quickly to the bag, and touched it for the third out.

"What grade is she in?" Eddie inquired, mildly impressed at her performance.

"I figure eighth or ninth," said Tip thoughtfully.

"Then she's about thirteen or fourteen."

"I'd say so."

14

The teams exchanged sides and Eddie watched to see if Monahan was going to bat. He was anxious to see how she did at the plate, too.

The first Surf grounded out to shortstop. The second drove a hot liner through the third baseman's legs and beat it on to second base.

"Hey, look who's stepping into the on-deck circle," Tip said. It was Phyl Monahan.

The guy at the plate took a called strike, waited out two pitches, then lined out to second. Two outs.

A cheer went up from the fans as Monahan stepped to the plate. She leaned the bat against her thigh, rubbed her hands a couple of times, then grabbed the bat and got set.

Tanglewood's pitcher was a tall left-hander with a fast overhand delivery. His first pitch to Phyl came in high, and she let it go. The next was even with her chest, and she swung at it. The crack of the bat was solid. The ball shot out to short center field, and she took off for first.

She could run. Her pigtails bobbed on her neck, and her shirt ballooned on her back as she sped to the bag. Her fans cheered her, letting her know they loved what she did.

Puffy looked at Eddie. "How'd you like to pitch to her?"

Eddie shrugged. "I don't know."

"You might have your chance."

"Not right away, I hope," he said.

There was just something about pitching to a girl that rankled.

"As soon as next Tuesday," said Puffy.

Eddie frowned. He took off his cap and ran his fingers through his dark, damp hair.

"I don't know. I just don't give a darn about pitching to a girl." He spoke his mind with honest conviction.

"Why not? Afraid that she'd get a hit off of you?" Puffy laughed.

"I just don't like the idea, that's all," said Eddie.

Deep inside, he felt that it might have something to do with what had caused his family to move to Florida. His father had been in line for a promotion in the company he was working for, but the job was given to a woman. Although Mr. Rhodes hardly ever complained about it, Eddie thought it wasn't fair. Now a girl was playing on a boys' team, taking a position away from a boy. Why did they have to butt in where they weren't welcome, anyway?

A kid walked, and Monahan went to second, taking long, swift steps, her arms swinging at her sides.

"Look at her," said Eddie critically. "She acts like she's it."

"How do you expect her to act?" said Tip. "She's doing well."

"Yes, but she thinks she's really something. I can tell."

"Maybe she is," Puffy cut in. "She's got to be, to be able to play with a bunch of guys."

Eddie kept his eye on her. She had reached the bag and was standing with one foot on it, the other on the ground.

"Maybe her father's got something to do with it," he said. "I've heard of families with only one daughter, and the father pushes her into something he'd been planning on a son to do."

"I don't know whether she's an only child or not," said Puffy. "Whatever she is, she isn't bad."

"But I wouldn't want her to play with us," Tip said.

"Neither would I," agreed Eddie. He looked at Puffy. "I suppose you would."

Puffy turned to him. "Who said so? I'm just saying she's not bad."

She scored easily on a drive to right center field.

"Let's go," suggested Tip.

"I'm ready," said Eddie.

They left the park and went home.

Eddie lived on Baker Avenue, a block away from Tip and three blocks away from Puffy. It was a relatively new neighborhood. Most of the homes were less than five years old. Some of the lawns looked like pictures cut out of *House and Garden* magazine.

Eddie found his mother paring potatoes at the kitchen sink.

"Hi, Mom," he greeted her. "What're you making for supper?"

"Steak and potatoes," she answered promptly. "Hamburg steak, that is."

She was short, brown-haired, and had a weight problem. Once a week she attended a weight-control class, but Eddie couldn't see that it was doing much good.

She had taken to the new town right away. Besides working with her husband at the gift shop, she was secretary of the Junior Women's League, a member of the church's women's auxiliary, and she sang in the choir.

"How'd you boys do?"

He took off his cap and headed toward the bathroom. "We won."

"Score?"

"Six–four."

He walked on past the bathroom, took a look inside the living room, and saw his sister Margie sprawled out on a chair. She was reading a teens' magazine.

"Hi," he said.

The magazine lowered below a pair of sharp, intelligent blue eyes. "Hi." Above the eyes was a head of straight dark hair that disappeared again as the magazine resumed its former position.

"Hey, pie face," said Eddie, "you know a girl named Monahan? Phyllis Monahan?"

The magazine lowered again, this time enough to reveal a button nose and a small, perky mouth. Margie was twelve.

"Phyl Monahan? Sure. Why?"

"What do you know about her?"

The eyes brightened with interest. "Not much. Except that she's popular. Why?"

"What do you mean, popular?"

"She's a nice kid. She's a brain. And she's got a lot of friends. Why?"

"Where does she live?"

"On Brenda Ave. Hey, what's going on? Why all this interest in Phyllis Monahan?"

"She plays first base for the Surfs."

Margie's eyes almost popped. "She what?"

Eddie smiled.

"See ya later," he said, waving to her. "I've got to wash this stinking sweat off."

3

Tip came over on his ten-speed bike after supper.
Eddie heard the sound of its bell from inside the
house and went out to meet him in the driveway. He
had one similar to Tip's, except that his was three
years old, and rust had begun to show.

"Where you heading?" asked Eddie.

Tip stood astride his bike and took off his bright
blue helmet.

"Thought we'd go for a spin and stop for some soft
ice cream," he replied. "You got enough dough? If
not, I—"

"Yeah, I've got enough," said Eddie.

"Good. Get your wheels."

Eddie went into the house and found his mother
cutting coupons out of a newspaper.

"Mom, Tip's here. Okay if I get my bike and go
with him for a spin?"

"Just get back before dark," she told him.

He grinned. "Don't I always?"

He hurried out to the garage, grabbed his helmet off a wall hook, and took out his bike. He was careful not to scrape it against his father's crimson-colored Thunderbird. One scratch on that baby and he might as well figure on being grounded for a week. His father had planned on owning a Thunderbird as long as five years ago and had had this one for only three months.

Eddie pulled down the door, got on the bike, and took off down the street after Tip.

They rode side by side, Eddie between Tip and the curb. Riding to Big Mike's Soft Ice Cream Shop was a regular ritual for them. But this time Eddie thought about taking a different route to it.

"Let's turn right on the next street," he suggested.

Tip looked at him. "Why?"

"Trust me," replied Eddie.

They reached the end of the block and turned right, both making the turn at precisely the same time. Eddie thought it would've made a neat picture if a photographer had been standing close by then.

"We're going out of our way, you know that?" Tip said.

"Not for long," said Eddie.

They rode on for six more blocks. Tip looked at Eddie again and wanted to know what he had on his mind to want to ride out of their way like this.

21

"Tell you later," Eddie promised, getting a kick out of keeping Tip in suspense.

Trees lined both sides of the street, providing plenty of shade for the elite-looking, two- and three-story homes. Cars were parked along the curb, most of them big and shiny, with spoke wheels, new tires, and vinyl tops.

They reached the intersection. Eddie looked to the left and right and saw a girl riding a three-speed bicycle. She was about halfway down the block. She had long, blond hair and was wearing a cap. She looked as if she were carrying something on one arm, and steering with the other.

"Tip!" shouted Eddie, recognizing her. "This way!"

He slowed down, made a sharp, right-hand turn, and headed up the street after the girl. He waited for Tip to catch up to him, then pedalled faster.

"Hey! Where you going?" Tip called after him.

Eddie smiled. "That's her," he said.

Tip frowned. "That's who?"

"Monahan."

"Monahan? You crazy? Is that why you wanted to come this way?"

They drew up fast behind her, Eddie leading the way. She was riding her bike near the right side of the street, but leaving enough space for Eddie to ride up between her and the curb.

He turned and motioned to Tip to ride up on the other side of her, trying to hide a mischievous smile that tugged at the corners of his mouth.

She was a ballplayer, right? She was one of the guys. Okay, let's see how she'd take to two guys riding shotgun with her. Eddie almost burst out laughing at the thought.

He saw her turn and look at him, her eyes widening. Then she turned and looked at Tip. Whatever it was — surprise at their sudden appearance, fear that they might run into her, or both — caused her to lose control of her bicycle.

She let out a scream as it started to weave. Both Eddie and Tip, seeing what was happening, pedalled harder. She lost her balance and fell, spilling the contents of a bag she was carrying. Onions, tomatoes, a head of lettuce, a box of salt, and a carton of eggs all hit the street, and everything that could roll, rolled. What couldn't, thumped, thudded, and then spilled over in a slimy yellow and white pattern on the street.

"Oh, no!" Phyl Monahan screamed. "You freaks! You dirty, awful freaks! Look what you made me do!"

Eddie wished he could turn time back. Of all the

23

dumb moves, this idea of taking a different route to Big Mike's, meeting Monahan, then riding up on both sides of her was the dumbest.

He stopped his bike next to her, kicked out the stand, and rushed over to her. Close by, Tip was doing the same thing, the expression on his face full of accusation and disgust. The look on his face said, "I hope you're satisfied, you jerk!"

"I'm sorry," Eddie said to Phyllis Monahan. "Geez, I'm sorry."

"Me, too," murmured Tip.

She stared at one of them and then the other, daggers shooting from her fiery blue eyes.

"Let me help you up," Eddie offered.

"Don't touch me!" she yelled, drawing away from him as if he were some kind of poisonous insect. "I'll help myself!"

While she started to unscramble herself from the bike and pick herself up, Eddie got the paper sack and started to refill it with the onions, the tomatoes, the head of lettuce, and the box of salt. Tip had picked up the egg carton and was replacing the few eggs that had managed to survive the accident.

"There are only four that were broken," he observed. "The rest look okay."

Phyl Monahan glared at him. "Only four?" she yelled. "Do you know how much eggs cost? But how would you? You probably know nothing about eggs except to eat them! Neither one of you look as if you've got an ounce of brains — "

She stopped as Eddie took out his imitation-leather coin purse and the folded dollar bill he had stashed in it. He'd been carrying it around for two weeks, waiting for something worthwhile to spend it on.

"Here," he said, unfolding it and handing it to her. "Take it. Here's also fifty cents. If that's not enough — "

"Here's my dollar, too," Tip cut in, unrolling a bill and holding it out to her.

She grabbed Eddie's. "One's enough," she said. Then she looked at the ugly blotch of smashed eggs on the street. "What a mess. You guys ought to be ashamed of yourselves."

"The rain will wash it away," said Eddie.

Monahan grabbed her bike, lifted it upright, and started to ride it away, but stopped suddenly when a loud, rubbing sound came from the front wheel.

"Oh, great!" she said sharply. "You've dented the fender. It's rubbing against the wheel."

"Maybe I can fix it," said Eddie. He stepped to the bike, grabbed the dented fender, and tried to pry it away from the wheel. It wouldn't budge.

"Who do you think you are?" Monahan snapped.

"Mr. Muscles? Walk it home for me. That's the least you can do."

Eddie looked at Tip. "Stay here with the bikes. I'll walk it home for her."

He walked it alongside her while she carried the bag of groceries. Halfway down the block she stepped into a driveway, turned, and looked at him.

"Lean it against the garage," she ordered, looking at him as if he were a kind of insect she didn't like. "And, thanks."

"You're welcome," he said, placing the bike where she had told him to. Then he ran back up the street to where Tip was waiting for him.

"Man!" he said. "What a woman!"

They got on their bikes and headed home. The heck with the ice cream, Eddie thought. He had lost his appetite for it. Even Tip, whose only fault was that he had gone along with Eddie's crazy idea, didn't care about having the stuff.

"I just don't understand why you wanted to go that way in the first place," Tip exclaimed as they took their time riding home.

"I just wanted to see where she lived. Her neighborhood," replied Eddie.

"But, why? What difference does it make?"

"No difference."

"You wanted to see what she looks like in jeans? Is that it?"

"No. I told you. I just wanted to see where she lived. That's all there is to it. Forget it. Okay?"

Tip could get real aggravating at times, he thought.

"You're crazy, you know that? You're really crazy, Eddie Rhodes."

Sometimes a guy does things he can't understand, Eddie told himself. If he can't understand why he does them, how can he explain them? He just can't.

They rode their bikes down the street to their homes, Eddie splitting first, giving a wave to Tip as Tip rode on.

It had turned out to be a very unsatisfying evening.

4

Harry Goldman pitched in the game against the Pirates. Eddie watched it from the bench, taking his turn to coach at first base at the top of the fourth inning.

He had hoped he would pitch, because whoever pitched today wouldn't be pitching next Tuesday. Coach Inger liked to alternate his pitchers just as he did his infielders and outfielders. He didn't carry more than a thirteen-man team, and alternated his infielders and outfielders in the same game.

The Pirates were leading 6–1. The Lancers had gotten five hits off Shifty McGoon, the Pirates' left-hander, but hadn't been able to bunch them together.

Eddie kept his eye on Coach Inger, noticing the tanned, knitted forehead, the intense, intelligent eyes. The coach still had hopes of lifting the Lancers out from under.

But how? Eddie wondered. He considered one possibility, but it was a slim one.

He's going to have me go in there, Eddie assumed. I can feel it. And I hope he does. Because then he would have me start against the Surfs next Tuesday, and have Harry finish it. Which would be fine with me. I don't want to pitch against that girl any more than I have to.

Eddie's guess was confirmed the next inning. Rod Bellow was coming to the plate in the top of the fifth when the coach asked Puffy to coach first and had Pete Turner, the second-string catcher, warm up Eddie.

By now Eddie didn't care whether he pitched or not. Unless something drastic happened to his pitching arm he was sure he'd be in the game against the Surfs. Even pitching four or five innings would mean he'd face Phyl Monahan at least twice.

They went to the bullpen behind the third-base bleachers. He began throwing them slowly, then gradually harder. His first fast pitch sailed off to the right and out of Pete's reach. It bounced near the fence and rolled toward the left-field foul line.

"Hey, man," Pete said. "Keep them in the batting zone, okay?"

"Sorry," said Eddie.

Pete started to chase after the ball, but some kid sitting by the fence went after it, picked it up, and threw it back to him.

Eddie threw in a few more, trying hard to maintain control. He had a strong arm, one of the strongest in the league, according to Coach Inger. The coach once said that Eddie could be the best pitcher in the league were it not for his wild pitches. All Eddie had to do was practice on his control and eventually he'd come around.

No one had to tell him he still had a long way to go.

He had thrown about twenty pitches when there was a shout from the stands, and a few seconds later Coach Inger appeared from around the corner of the third-base bleachers.

"Eddie! Come on."

Eddie tossed the ball back to Pete and went around the bleachers to the mound. He accepted a brand-new ball from the umpire, waited for Tip to get on his gear, then began throwing in warmup pitches.

The plate umpire turned to face the crowd. "Pitching for the Lancers — Eddie Rhodes!"

"Yaaaaay!" sang the fans.

He had trouble finding the strike zone with the Pirates' first batter, and walked him. He was more careful with the next. He didn't throw too hard, and the batter hit into a double play. He struck out the third batter on a pitch that might've been called a ball, but the guy was too eager to hit and lashed at poor pitches.

Puffy met Eddie near the base path between home and third as they headed in toward the dugout. A teasing grin played on his round face.

"Well, buddy boy, looks like you're going in against the Surfs next week."

"Yeah." A dismal look came over Eddie's face.

"And Monahan," Puffy added.

"Monahan? Who's Monahan?"

Puffy laughed. "As if you didn't know."

They reached the dugout, and Eddie tossed his glove under the bench, turned, and sat down.

Tip came in, the buckles of his shin guards clanking. He smiled at Eddie through the smudges of sweaty dirt that covered his face.

"That last batter really went for your wild ones, didn't he?"

"An eager beaver," agreed Eddie. "That's the kind I like."

He moved over to give Tip room. Tip sat down, the seat of his pants caked with dirt.

"Good thing you've got me catching you or that

fence behind home plate would be in big trouble," said Tip.

Eddie tapped him on the knee. "What're you squawking about? I've only walked one guy, haven't I?"

"Yes. But unless you start getting that ball down near the strike zone you'll be walking the crowd."

They picked up two runs. It was now 6–3, in favor of the Pirates.

Eddie remembered Tip's warning when he got back on the mound and tried his best to groove his pitches. Nonetheless, he gave up a hit and walked a man, almost hitting him on the shoulder with his fourth pitch.

The Pirates picked up one run that inning. It was the only one either team managed to score the rest of the game.

Pirates 7, Lancers 3.

"We played lousy," Puffy grumbled as he, Tip, and Eddie headed through the gate for home. "Like a bunch of little kids who never had a ball in their hands."

"I hope we do better against the Surfs," said Tip.

Eddie looked at him. "Why do you have to keep mentioning the Surfs?"

"We're playing them next week, that's why."

"We know that. You don't have to keep reminding us."

Tip frowned. "Man, are you touchy. What did you have for lunch? Hot salami?"

"Don't you get it?" Puffy cut in. "Monahan plays with the Surfs. And it's a ninety-nine percent chance that he'll be pitching."

Tip laughed. "I know, I know. The last thing in the world old buddy Eddie wants is to pitch to a girl." He turned and patted Eddie gingerly on the back. "Well, old buddy, might as well stand up to the situation like a man. When she gets up to the plate just pretend she's another guy. She's going to wear a uniform like the rest of her team. If you're better than she is, you'll get her out in three pitches. Maybe less. If you aren't better —"

Eddie raised a hand. "Just one cotton-pickin' minute," he interrupted. "You two twerps don't seem to understand. She's a *girl*. And I don't think it's right for a girl to play in a boys' league. It's meant for us, don't you understand? She could be darn good. Heck, my sister Margie could play better baseball than a lot of guys in our league, but does that qualify her to play with us? No!"

"Like I said," said Tip calmly, "she's already on a team. No matter what you say or do you won't change that."

"Right," agreed Puffy. "But I'm with you, Eddie. I don't think a girl should play on a boys' team, either."

"What's your reason?" asked Tip, turning to him. "The same as Eddie's? Because she's a *girl?*"

Puffy nodded. "And girls get hurt easier. They're more fragile."

"Baloney," said Tip.

Eddie stared at him. "I suppose you think it's okay for a girl to play on a boys' team?"

Tip shrugged. "Look, if she's good, why not? If she gets hurt it's her own tough luck. She asked for it. She must've gotten permission from her parents to play. They must've signed for her. Otherwise she wouldn't be playing."

"I still say she's a girl," said Eddie, refusing to yield to his friend's arguments. "And girls shouldn't — "

"Let's knock it off," Puffy broke in irritably. "There must be something better to talk about than a girl playing on a boys' baseball team."

"What about love?" Tip suggested, smiling.

"Hey, that's an idea," said Puffy. "You suppose she knows anything about *that?*"

"Love? Her?" Eddie sneered. "You've seen her face. She looks as if she grew up on hay."

Puffy and Tip laughed.

None of them had much to say about anything during the rest of their journey home.

There were times during the next few days that Eddie wished Tuesday would never come. He was almost one hundred percent certain that he was going to pitch against the Surfs, and a thought that had crossed his mind, one that he had not mentioned to a living soul, was the possibility of Phyllis Monahan's getting a hit off him — or maybe two. He remembered Puffy's teasing him, "Afraid that she'd get a hit off of you?" If she was as great a hitter as some of the guys on his team said she was, she might wind up with an extra baser. He didn't want to think what that would do to his ego.

Damn! Guys should never be shown up by girls, he thought. Why couldn't she have found a girls' baseball team to play on?

But he knew why, of course. Argus didn't have a girls' baseball team. It had girls' softball teams, but apparently good ol' Phyl Monahan thought she was too good to play on one of them.

Tuesday rolled around quicker than he wished, and Eddie learned for certain that a part of his fears was turning out true. He was starting.

While the Lancers were playing catch near the first-base side of the ball park, the Surfs were taking their batting practice. Eddie tried to pretend he didn't care who batted, but from the corner of his eye he furtively watched to see when Phyl Monahan would come up to the plate.

She was the fifth to bat. This might or might not mean she was fifth in the batting lineup. But when Tip laid his mitt against his hip to take time out to watch her bat, Eddie found it was an excellent excuse for him to watch her, too.

A quick glimpse at the other Lancer players showed that they all were curious about her ability. Did she rate with the rest of her teammates, or didn't she?

She let the first pitch go by, hit the next one down to shortstop, the next to center field, and the next two to deep left. The last drive hit the top of the fence, missed clearing it by inches, and bounced back onto the field.

Eddie turned away, not caring to see how well she could bunt.

"Hey, you see that?" Tip exclaimed, taking the mitt from his hip and resuming play.

Eddie grunted, preferring not to pursue the topic any further.

Tip smiled, as if he understood.

After the Surfs finished their batting practice, the Lancers took their turn. Lynn drilled a liner that hit the center-field fence, and Dale lambasted one a few feet over it, the only two long drives hit among the Lancers' thirteen players.

From the quiet of their dugout the Lancers watched the Surfs work out in field practice, their attention drawn mainly to the kid playing first base. Phyl Monahan.

"She's got a mean stretch," Puffy observed. "Watch her, Rod. Maybe you can learn something."

"Bull," scoffed Rod.

Monahan reached for a high throw, and pulled it down.

"See that?" said Lynn. "Half the time her foot's off the bag."

She pegged it back across the diamond.

"Throws like a girl," said Paul.

"She is a girl, dummy," said Tip. "Or don't you know the difference?"

Coach Inger stepped up in front of them in time to hear the exchange of remarks.

"Okay, cut the sarcasm," he snapped, and looked at Eddie. "How's the arm, pal?"

"Okay."

"Good." He looked over his shoulder. "They're coming off. Okay, get out there, and let's take them."

5

Eddie grooved the first pitch and watched it go for a sharp single over Paul's head.

"Not too good, Eddie, boy!" Rod said.

"Breeze it by 'im, Eddie!" said Larry, stepping up on the grass near the third-base sack.

Eddie caught the relay from Puffy, who was covering second base, and stepped back on the mound. He waited for the next Surf batter to get into the box, studied him a moment, and nodded his agreement to Tip's sign.

He streaked one toward the inside of the plate. The batter started to put his bat out to bunt, then quickly jumped back to avoid being hit.

"Ball!" shouted the ump.

"Make it be in there, Eddie!" cried Paul. "Make it be in there!"

He made it be in there, and this time the batter successfully stuck out his bat for a neat bunt inside the third-base line. Larry came in, pounced on it, and pulled his arm back to throw.

"Second base!" Eddie yelled.

On the verge of throwing to first, Larry threw to second instead. Paul, covering the bag, stretched to catch the throw, but the runner beat it by a step.

"No!" cried the base umpire, giving the safe sign.

Tip glared at Eddie. "Dummy, why'd you tell him to throw to second? He was too far away from it!"

Eddie shook his head, aware now he should have kept his mouth shut. "I thought he had time," he said lamely.

"Sure you did," grumbled Tip.

Eddie read the sarcasm in Tip's voice and tried to ignore it. Sometimes it wasn't hard to irk the burly catcher, especially when he felt he was right on an important play.

Eddie caught the soft throw from Paul, took a look at the men on first and second, and stepped on the mound.

Tip signaled for a curve and gave him a target on the inside of the plate. Eddie threw it. The ball headed toward the inside corner and dipped in. The batter swung. Missed.

"Strike one!" snapped the ump.

Tip gave him the two-finger sign again. Eddie nodded, stretched, and pitched. The ball headed for the middle of the plate. Just as it dipped toward the outside corner, the batter swung. The fat part of the bat connected with the ball and sent it flying toward short right field.

Eddie watched it drop on the grass, a sick feeling coming to his stomach. The hit was going to knock in one run at least, he thought.

Right fielder Tony Netro bolted after it, grabbed it on the second hop, and pegged it home. The runner on second made the turn at third and was a quarter of the way home when Tip caught the ball.

He probably decided he couldn't make it, because he hightailed it back, diving under Tip's throw to third. He was safe.

Larry carried the ball halfway over to Eddie then tossed it the other half.

"Watch for a squeeze, Larry," Eddie cautioned.

Eddie watched a tall, well-built cleanup hitter come to the plate, and glanced at the batter stepping into the on-deck circle. It was Monahan.

For a second their eyes met, and he looked away, staring at the grass as he headed back toward the mound. He was sure she recognized him and Tip as the guys who had caused her to lose her balance on her bicycle that day last week.

Tip called time and trotted in toward him. They met in front of the mound.

"What do you want to do?" Tip asked.

Eddie frowned. "What do you mean?"

"I think he'll try to squeeze in a run."

"Shall I keep them high?"

"Yeah. But not too high. I don't want to be jumping for them."

Eddie smiled. "You won't."

Tip returned to his position. The ump called time in. Eddie walked onto the mound and set his left foot on the rubber. His first pitch was even with the batter's face. The batter tried a bunt and ticked it.

"Strike!" said the ump.

Eddie placed the next pitch high and inside. The batter swerved to avoid being hit.

"Ball!" said the ump.

"In there, Eddie," Tip encouraged him. "In there, boy."

Eddie grooved the next pitch. He hadn't intended to; it just happened that way.

The batter bunted. The ball dropped in front of the plate and rolled toward the pitcher's mound. Eddie sped after it, aware that the runner on third was blazing for home. He reached the ball, scooped it up, and tossed it underhand to Tip.

"Ouuuut!" yelled the ump as Tip tagged the sliding runner.

Cheers exploded from the Lancer fans.

"Nice play, Eddie!"

"Way to go, Eddie, boy!"

Tip came toward him, smiling, and tapped the ball into his glove. "Look who's up."

"I know."

"Think she'll bunt?"

"With one out?" Eddie shrugged.

He turned and headed back toward the mound.

"Send it out of the lot, Phyl!" yelled a Surf player from the dugout.

"Clear the bases, Phyl!" yelled another.

Eddie took time to size up the situation. There was one out, the bases were loaded, and Phyllis Monahan was up. In a million years he wouldn't have dreamed he'd be in a position like this. Facing a girl batter upset him enough. To be facing her with the bases loaded multiplied his anxiety tenfold.

Suppose — just *suppose* — that she got a lucky hit off him? One, or two, or even three runs could score. What would a freak thing like that do to him? Talk about humiliation!

"Get 'er out of there, Eddie, boy!" Rod said in a steady chatter from first base. "Get 'er out of there, boy!"

He stepped on the mound, absently ran his arm across his forehead, and took a quick glance at the sweat he had wiped off. He couldn't believe it. She was making him sweat.

I'm going to strike you out, Monahan, he promised

42

silently. I'm going to show you that girls don't belong on a boys' team.

"Put it here, baby!" Tip yelled, tapping the pocket of his mitt with his fist. "Right here, baby!"

Eddie stretched, and delivered. The ball streaked for the outside corner, missed it by an inch. Monahan let it go.

"Ball!" said the ump.

"Make it be in there, Eddie!" said Paul.

Eddie let go another. This one started to cut the inside corner, and Monahan swung. The sound of bat meeting ball was solid. The ball shot out to left field, a high, arcing drive that looked as if it might go over the fence. The yell that started from the Surfs' fans began to grow and grow.

Eddie watched the ball, his breath caught in his throat. The white dot kept curving, kept curving toward the left, and finally struck the fence about five feet left of the foul line.

"Foul!" yelled the home-plate umpire.

The fans' yell changed from one of hope to a groan of disappointment.

Cries deluged him. "Hey, man! Are you lucky!"

"She's got your number, Eddie!"

"What do you think of *that* power for a girl, Eddie?"

He tried to ignore them. It was a lucky hit, he told

himself. The pitch was just right for her. Waist high. Inside corner. She'd be a lousy hitter if she *hadn't* hit it, foul or not.

The ump handed Tip a new ball. Tip tossed it to Eddie. Eddie rubbed it around in his hands. He always liked the feel of a new ball. It felt as if it were his own, that he could control its destiny.

The ump stretched out his arms and held out a finger from each hand to show the crowd the count.

Tip signaled for a curve. Eddie's nod was almost imperceptible. He stretched and threw.

The ball shot toward the inside of the plate, and high. Monahan started to lean into it, pulling her bat back in readiness to swing.

Suddenly her eyes widened in fear. She started to turn her head, to duck away from the incoming pitch. Eddie froze as he saw the direction the ball was taking. *It wasn't going where he intended it to! It was streaking for her head!*

"Duck!" he shouted. "Duck!"

She tried, but the throw was too fast for her, too close. The ball struck her in the back of her head. It glanced off her helmet and bounced high into the air, landing near the backstop screen.

She collapsed in the batter's box, and didn't move.

6

Eddie stared, mouth open, frozen. He saw Tip standing by the plate, staring at the fallen batter as if he were stricken, too.

The plate umpire was the first one to reach her. He knelt beside her, clutched her hand, talked to her. He was nervous, worried. The two base umpires were running forward, too.

Players poured out from both dugouts.

"Hold it!" Coach Inger commanded his men. "You guys stay here!"

The Surfs' coach was running toward his girl star, oblivious to his team's running close at his heels. Fear and anxiety filled their faces and eyes.

Eddie heard the word "ambulance," and saw one of the base umpires heading toward the narrow opening between the backstop screen and the Lancers' dugout.

He stood awhile, immobilized, feeling as if he were watching a scene on television.

He saw Surf players glare accusingly at him.

"You did it on purpose, Rhodes," a red-haired kid snapped at him.

"Yeah," snarled another, lips drawn up at the corners.

A kid came running from the third-base bleachers, a tall, big-boned kid with dark hair and wild eyes, fists clenched.

"You louse!" he shouted at Eddie, ready to swing at him. "You were jealous of her and you hit her! You hit her on purpose!"

He swung, catching Eddie by surprise, and hit him on the side of the jaw. Eddie saw an explosion of stars and reeled.

"You crumb!" the kid raved on. "I'll —"

"Hey, cut it out!" another voice broke in.

Eddie saw Larry and Puffy grab the big kid from behind. Rod came to help and tried to pin the kid's arms to his back. The kid was strong, and anger seemed to boost his strength as he pulled himself free from the three boys and started back after Eddie.

Eddie stood there, his fists clenched and held up now to protect himself.

"I didn't!" he cried. "I didn't do it on purpose! I would never throw at a batter intentionally!"

The kid swung at him again, and Eddie caught the blow on his arm.

"You did then, you rat!" the kid yelled. "You did *that* intentionally!"

"No! You've got to believe me!"

A cop came bolting toward them. He reached the big kid, grabbed his right arm, and twisted it behind his back.

"All right, now," he said in a calm voice. "Settle down."

He held the kid till his anger had subsided. Then he slowly took his arms from around him.

"Take off," the cop ordered, shoving him away. "Get back in the bleachers. I don't care what you do, but keep away from him."

The kid gave him a mean look and turned again to Eddie.

"She's my cousin," he rasped. "I'm going to see that you don't get away with it, head buster."

The cop grabbed his shoulders. "I said take off, buddy. I don't want to keep repeating myself. Okay?"

The kid said nothing. He shrugged his shoulders and started toward the bleachers. Then he changed his mind and headed toward the small group that had assembled near the prostrate girl.

Her bare head was lying on the dirt.

"She ought to have something under her head," Eddie said to the cop.

The cop looked at the girl. "No one's supposed to touch her," he said. "The ambulance will be here in a minute. The medics will handle it. They know what to do."

A siren whirred in the distance. In seconds a blue-and-white ambulance swept into the park, lights flashing. The siren quieted down to a dead silence. The lights kept blinking. Two men in white uniforms broke out of the vehicle and rushed to the girl. One took her hand, felt her pulse, pulled back an eyelid and looked at her eye. The other took a look at her, then raced back to the ambulance, and brought out a stretcher. They lifted the girl onto it and put her inside the ambulance. A woman got in with her. Her mother, Eddie figured.

The ambulance sped off.

Coach Inger looked around, saw Eddie standing by the mound, and came over to him. He squinted against the sun and put a hand on Eddie's shoulder.

"Don't worry. She'll be all right."

Eddie felt a lump in his throat. "I didn't do it on purpose," he said.

"Who said you did?"

He looked at the Surf players. "They do. And her cousin."

The coach frowned. "The kid who went after you? I saw him. If the cop hadn't come just then, I would have." He looked at Eddie's jaw. "Did he hurt you?"

"No."

The base umpire came toward them. "Sam, you ready to go?"

The coach nodded. "Anytime." He turned back to Eddie. "Don't feel too bad about hitting her. The ball must've struck her head on a vulnerable spot. That's why you wear helmets, to avoid accidents just like that one. It may never happen again in a hundred years."

"But it did happen to her," said Eddie thinly.

"One of those things," said the coach. "Take a load off your feet. I'll have Harry pitch."

Eddie walked off the field, still half-dazed. He entered the dugout and sat down. He folded his glove, crossed his arms over his chest, and wondered whether to stay and watch the rest of the game, or go home.

He wanted desperately to go home, to put the ball game and the tragic accident far behind him. He might as well, he thought. He couldn't get back into the game, even if the Surfs pounded Harry all over the lot. All he'd do was think about that wild pitch that had bounced off Phyllis Monahan's head.

But something in his conscience reminded him that going home now would be cowardly. It would be like a soldier running away from the field of battle.

He stayed.

Being hit by a pitched ball had entitled Monahan to a walk, so a kid took first base in her place, forcing in a run. Eddie watched two more runs score on a line drive over second base.

The Lancers settled down finally and got the Surfs out — one, two, three.

Puffy came in and sat down beside him. Tip sat on his other side.

"You okay?" Puffy asked.

"Yeah."

"If you want to go home you can," said Tip. "You don't have to wait for me."

"I'm staying," said Eddie.

The game remained close all the way. The Lancers finally won it, 5–4.

What difference did it make who won? All that counted was that he had hit Phyl Monahan, Eddie thought.

When he started off the field, his sister Margie came off the stands and rushed to him. She grabbed his hand and looked up into his face.

"I saw that kid hit you," she said resentfully. "Why should he blame you for hitting that girl? You didn't do it on purpose. I know you didn't."

He smiled and squeezed her hand. "He's her cousin, and I guess he thought I did."

Tip and Puffy joined them. They exchanged greetings with Margie.

Suddenly Eddie saw a familiar face in the crowd. Speak of the devil, he thought. The stern, angry eyes focused on him.

"There he is," he said to Tip. "Look. He's still sore."

Tip looked in the direction Eddie was looking. "Yeah," he said. "I guess he is. If looks could kill, you'd be dead."

"Do you know him?"

"No. Never saw him before today."

They arrived home, and Tip and Puffy split. His older sister, Roxie, was alone in the house. She was a senior in high school and, like their mother, had dark hair and was a bit on the heavy side.

"Hi, Rox," Eddie greeted her. "You ready to leave?"

"Yes."

Their parents worked at the gift shop from nine A.M. till five P.M. She took over from five till eight-thirty P.M.

Her forehead knitted into a tight frown as she looked from Eddie to Margie. "What's with you two?" she asked wonderingly. "You both look as if the world's turned upside down. Was the score that bad?"

Eddie started to fumble with the buttons on his jersey. "The way we look has nothing to do with the score."

"Oh? What happened?"

He told her, from top to bottom, while she listened, wide-eyed and concerned. When he finished, she said, "How awful. Do you know how seriously hurt she is?"

"No." He paused. "I think I'd like to go to the hospital and see her."

"When?"

"After I change and eat." He watched for her reaction. He had accepted the fact long ago that she was older, smarter, and had more mature judgment than he. Since both his mother and father were at the gift shop most of the day, he saw his sister a lot and found her dependable when he needed her opinion on important matters.

Her forehead furrowed for a moment, then smoothed out again.

"If she's badly hurt they might not let you see her."

He thought a moment. "You think it's okay, though, that I go to see her?"

"Yes. I not only think it's okay, I think it's a good idea. I would if I were in your place."

He smiled. "Thanks, Rox."

He took off his uniform, washed, and put on a clean pair of pants and a shirt. Roxie fixed him and Margie a dish of fish and chips, then left, saying that she was late already in relieving their mother and father.

"See you guys later," she said as she flew out of the door and to her car.

Later, Eddie rode his bike to the hospital, parked it in the lot, and walked on the sidewalk to the front entrance. He entered, advanced nervously to the reception desk, and stood there until the gray-haired, matronly woman turned to look at him.

"Can I help you?" she asked.

He cleared his throat. "Can I see Phyllis Monahan?"

The woman's blue eyes focused on him. "Phyllis Monahan? Just a minute."

She riffled through a stack of index cards, stopped at one, then picked up the telephone and dialed a number. After a few seconds she spoke softly into it, listened briefly, smiled at the card she was holding, said "Thank you," and hung up.

"I'm sorry," she told Eddie. "But no one can see Miss Monahan right now except her parents. She's in intensive care."

He looked worried.

"Does — does that mean she's badly hurt?" he asked anxiously.

She shrugged her hefty shoulders. "I don't know what her actual condition is. Even if I did, I couldn't say." She smiled warmly. "Why don't you call back later?"

"Later tonight?"

She nodded. "Or tomorrow morning."

He felt a draft of cool air sweep in from outside as the front door opened and a chattering group came in. Suddenly the babble of voices stopped.

"Hey, look!" A single voice suddenly evolved from the mixture. "Isn't that him?"

He turned and saw four girls in blue jeans and colored blouses standing in front of the door. It remained open as long as they stood on the electrically activated walk. Four pairs of eyes focused on him accusingly.

"It is him," one of the other girls said. "Of all the nerve."

He sucked in his breath, let it out slowly, and looked back at the receptionist. "Thank you," he said, and started toward the exit.

He felt glaring eyes on him. Near the door he had to wait for one of the girls to move aside to permit him to pass.

"Turkey!" she flung at him as he stepped out.

7

His mother's and father's car was in the garage when Eddie got home. He pulled open the door, rode his bike inside, popped out the stand, then left, closing the door behind him.

He went into the house through the back door and found his mother in the kitchen, doing the dishes. Margie was helping her.

"Sorry about the dishes, Mom," he said. "I planned on doing them when I —"

She looked at him. "That's okay. Margie told me. Did you see the girl?"

"No. She's in intensive care."

His mother's face paled. Margie glanced curiously from him to her. "Intensive care? What's that, Mom?"

"That means she must've been seriously hurt," her mother explained. "Oh, dear, I hope it's not *too* serious."

She started to rinse the suds off a dish, but it

slipped out of her hands and dropped back into the water. Nervously she grabbed it up again, and this time managed to hold it firmly while she rinsed it under the faucet.

"Where's Dad?" he asked.

"In the living room." Her mouth twitched, and flecks of pink touched her cheeks. "Eddie?"

"Yes, Mom?"

"Was she wearing a helmet?"

"Yes. We all have to when we bat. She turned and ducked when she saw the ball coming at her, and it hit her in the back of the head. It probably just missed her helmet. I don't know."

She put the dish in the plastic drainer. "You've got to be careful about pitching, Eddie. Margie told me you're kind of wild. Maybe you should play some other position."

"It's too late to think about that now, Mom. I've got to get over this worry first."

"I know."

He went into the living room and heard the familiar voice of a news announcer blaring from the television set. His father was sitting in the armchair across from it, all rapt attention.

"Hi, Dad," Eddie greeted him.

"Hi, son," his father answered without turning away from the set. "Look at that. The market's still dipping. Wall Street's still worried about the oil situation. I don't know. Maybe I ought to talk to my broker."

Eddie watched the initials moving across the top of the TV screen in alphabetical order, the current market value per share under them. Watching the market report was one of his father's daily rituals.

"Dad," Eddie started to say.

"Not now, Eddie," his father said. "Later. Okay?"

Eddie's heart sank. "Okay," he said.

He sat down on the couch and waited till his father was finished watching the report. When it was over, he started to say again, "Dad, can I — "

His father looked sternly at him. "Can it wait till after the news, Eddie?"

Eddie shrugged. "Yeah. Well, anyway, it's not important."

He got off the couch and headed for the door. He hoped his father would call to him, stop him, and ask him what he wanted. But his father didn't, so he opened the door and walked out.

The cool air hit his face, refreshing him. He walked around the block, hoping to see Tip or Puffy or one of the other guys from his team. But he didn't. It was dusk by the time he got back. He sat on the porch and thought about telephoning the hospital to see how Phyllis Monahan was, but he decided to postpone it till tomorrow. It was dark when he went back into the house.

Later that night he sat in his bedroom and looked dreamily at his drums. He had a set of snares and a bass that he banged away on every once in a while. Sometimes he'd play it when he was depressed. It would give him a lift; make him forget his little problems.

But he didn't feel like playing it at all now, and he couldn't be more depressed. Maybe if Tip came over with his trumpet he'd get out of it, but he didn't feel like calling Tip up, either.

The next morning he telephoned the hospital at eleven o'clock to see how Phyllis Monahan was. The receptionist who answered said that she was still in the intensive-care unit.

He didn't go to practice that afternoon. Just before supper Tip came over and said that the coach had asked about him.

"Did he hear anything about Monahan?" Eddie inquired.

"I guess not," Tip replied. "He didn't say anything about her."

At suppertime Eddie didn't ladle half as much food onto his plate as he usually did. His father noticed his apparent lack of appetite and asked him, "Hey, fella, on a diet?"

Eddie shrugged. "No. I just don't feel like eating very much."

His father frowned.

"Are you worried about the girl you hit while pitching yesterday?"

Eddie nodded.

"Why didn't you tell me about it?" his father demanded, fixing his eyes firmly on Eddie's. "I didn't know until your mother mentioned it to me last night."

Eddie found it hard swallowing a forkful of potatoes, and tried to avoid his father's eyes. "I tried to tell you about it while you were watching the news last night," he said thinly.

His father nodded. "Was that when I interrupted you and told you to wait till after the news?"

"Yes."

"Well, for Pete's sake, why didn't you tell me then?"

Eddie swallowed the food and took a deep breath. His stomach felt tight.

"I don't know."

"You don't know? That's a good answer. Since when has a girl played in your league, anyway?"

"Since the season started," Eddie answered.

"Well, I'm sorry she got hit, but girls shouldn't try to play in the same league with boys."

"Yeah." Eddie shrugged.

"Well, don't worry about her. She'll be all right."

Eddie put his fork down and sat back on his chair. He wasn't full; he just didn't feel like eating any more.

"But I do worry about her, Dad," he said emphatically. "I hit her, and the blow must've been serious because they put her in the intensive-care unit. Everybody thinks I hit her on purpose."

"Not everybody," said his mother.

"Well, her friends do, her teammates do, and her cousin does."

He wiped his mouth with a napkin, excused himself, and left the table.

"You only ate part of your supper," his mother said, glancing at the food he had left on his plate.

"I'm sorry, Mom," he said. "I just can't eat any more."

He went out to the backyard and lay on the hammock. It was his father's favorite relaxing place. Thoughts of Phyllis, of her friends, her cousin, and her parents streamed through his mind. The more he thought about them the more worried he became.

He rolled off the hammock, got his bike out of the garage, and rode over to Phyllis's house. If he couldn't find out how Phyllis was from anybody at the hospital, her parents should be able to tell him.

Nervous and frightened at the kind of reception he might receive from them, he rapped on the door. No one answered. He rapped again. Still no one answered. He realized then that her parents were probably visiting her at the hospital.

He got on his bike and headed there. He had a block to go when he started to pass by a florist.

Flowers, he thought, slowing down the bike. People always take flowers to someone who's ill. It's a good way of showing you care about them.

He rode into the parking lot, locked up his bike, and entered the shop. He looked around at the array of flowers, smelled their fragrance, and approached one of the small arrangements set inside a vase.

Twelve-fifty. He read the price label silently. Oh, wow, he thought. At that price he might as well forget about getting flowers.

A clerk came in from the greenhouse behind the shop, and for five minutes she offered suggestions about the kind of flowers to buy for a friend in the hospital. The various costs she always came up with far exceeded what he had in his pocket, so he finally thanked her and left.

He hadn't given up on the idea of taking flowers to Phyllis, however, so he returned home, picked some of the dahlias from his mother's garden, and rode back to the hospital. He locked the bike in the bike rack, went into the building, and faced the same receptionist he had met yesterday evening.

"Hi," she said, recognizing him, too. "How are you this evening?"

"Fine. Is Phyllis Monahan still in the intensive-care unit?"

"Just a minute. I'll check," she said.

She picked up a card from the pile she had in front of her and looked at it. "No. She's out of intensive care and in a ward room now. But there are already two people visiting her. Would you care to wait?"

He thought about it a moment. He felt sure the visitors were her parents. His courage deserted him.

"No, I don't think so," he said nervously. He held up the flowers. "Can you get these to her?"

She smiled. "Of course." She stood and took the bouquet from him. "I'll put them in a vase with water and have someone take them to her."

"Thanks."

"Who shall I say left them?" she wanted to know.

He thought about that, too.

"I'm not sure," he said.

"How about your name?"

"No." She might throw them into a basket if she heard the flowers came from him. "Just say that they're from a friend," he said.

8

At two o'clock Friday, Eddie and Tip rode their bikes to the ball field and parked them next to the first-base dugout. Coach Inger was already there, knocking flies out to the outfielders.

"Eddie, get out there," he ordered, after the boys put on their baseball shoes.

"Oh-oh," Tip muttered. "I guess he's going to put you in the outfield."

"Far out where no one can see me," replied Eddie.

He gathered up his glove and ran to the outfield. Dale, Lynn, Tony, and Tom were already out there, bunched in a spot in center field. Tony and Tom wore sunglasses to protect their eyes against the hot, glaring sun.

"Hi, Eddie," Dale greeted. "What're you doing out here?"

"Yeah, man," chimed in Lynn, squinting against the sun. "This is ball-shaggin' country."

"Aren't you going to pitch anymore?" Tony inquired.

"I don't know," said Eddie.

"Heads up, Eddie!" yelled Coach Inger.

Eddie braced himself. He watched the coach wallop the ball, and followed it with his eyes as it soared high toward him.

"Back up, Eddie. Back up," Dale advised.

He backtracked, stumbled, and lost sight of the ball. Dismay swept through him. Frantically he searched the blue sky for it, found it again, and rushed back. At the last moment he stopped and sprang ahead, realizing he had terribly misjudged it, and saw the ball strike the ground five feet in front of him.

"You're way off, Eddie," Lynn informed him.

"Try it again, Eddie!" Coach Inger yelled.

The next fly was just as high as the first one, and just as difficult to judge. It seemed to shrink in size again as it reached its zenith, and Eddie almost lost sight of it. When it began to drop, it seemed to waver in the air and dropped a foot behind him.

"You're getting better, Eddie, boy," Tony remarked, grinning.

The others laughed at him as he picked up the ball and heaved it in.

"Once more!" yelled the coach.

He didn't hit this one as high, nor as far. Eddie had

to sprint in after it. He stopped suddenly and caught the ball at his midriff.

"Nice catch, Eddie!" came Dale's cry from behind him.

He was out there for half an hour, taking turns with the other guys in catching fly balls. He missed more than he caught, and visualized himself as a steady bench warmer and a part-time outfielder.

"Didn't you ever play in the outfield?" Coach Inger asked him as he came in with the other players. "You look green as that grass out there."

Eddie took off his cap and wiped his forehead. He felt miserable. If he couldn't play in the outfield, he had little chance of playing at all. "No. I've just played a little at first base," he confessed.

"We've got a good first baseman," the coach replied. "As a matter of fact, we're in good shape all around except at pitching."

"And I guess it looks like you don't need me," Eddie declared.

He turned away so that the coach couldn't see the hurt look on his face. He wanted to pitch more than anything, but if he couldn't, he'd play any other position on the diamond if the coach would let him.

But the situation looked grim. Coach Inger just admitted that his infield was in good shape. He didn't have to say that his outfield was too, but Eddie knew it was. He felt like the hero in a story he had read recently, *The Man Without a Country*. Was he going to be the kid without a ball team?

"You just keep showing up," Coach Inger suggested. "We'll be losing Dale and Tony this year, and I'd like to make sure we'll have some starters in the outfield in our club next year. I don't want you to give up pitching, either. This is your second year with us and you're doing fine. You have a good arm, and your control isn't bad. Your big problem is losing concentration and throwing the ball far off your target. Lick that, and you'll be a fine pitcher."

He turned to the other members of his team. "Okay, infielders!" he yelled. "Get out there! Hustle!"

Eddie watched Rod, Paul, Puffy, and Larry run out to their positions, and felt envious. If he couldn't pitch anymore he'd prefer to work out as an infielder. He'd rather play infield than outfield, because he felt that there was more action there. And another thing: an infielder wasn't expected to hit as well as an outfielder. And he was no hitter. Put him in the outfield and he'd be as useful as a donkey.

"Eddie, grab a mitt," said the coach. "Work out with Harry awhile, then change gloves with him and pitch to him awhile. Okay?"

"Sure."

He put on a catcher's mitt, walked in front of the third-base bleachers with the team's southpaw pitcher, and worked him out. After about ten minutes they exchanged gloves and positions, and Eddie pitched. He tried hard to concentrate on each throw, but twice he sailed one far wide of the simulated plate, and once sent one zooming too far over Harry's head for him to reach.

"You're wild, man," declared Harry, shaking his head after that third wild throw. "You're really wild."

Eddie pursed his lips and fought hard to control his resentment.

"I know," he blurted. "You don't have to rub it in."

During batting practice, Eddie's hits were weak blows that would be easy outs in a ball game. Only one sailed out to the outfield, high enough to give the center fielder ample time to get under it.

He felt that his day was wasted. Practice had gained him nothing but a sick feeling in the pit of his stomach.

"Don't forget the game Tuesday," Coach Inger reminded the team as they got ready to break up and leave.

"Who we playing, Coach?" Rod asked.

"The Sidewinders. What's the matter? Don't you look at your schedule?"

"Lost mine," Rod replied.

The coach shook his head. "Meet me at the car. I've got a couple of extra ones."

Tip socked Eddie lightly on the shoulder. "Let's go."

They laid their shoes in the baskets of their bikes and rode off.

"What you hear about Monahan?" Tip asked Eddie.

"She's out of intensive care," Eddie answered.

"That's all?"

"Yeah."

They rode down the tree-lined, shadow-dappled street, tires singing. Tip's asking about Monahan reminded Eddie of the flowers he had left for her. Had she had any friends visiting her whom she might've asked about the flowers? he wondered. And, could she ever have figured out that they came from him?

His thoughts were interrupted by a car driving up behind them. A green coupe. From his rearview mirror he could see it coming closer to him, with no apparent intention of passing, even though the street was clear.

"Hey, what the heck is that guy trying to do?" he called to Tip.

Tip looked behind him. "I don't know!"

Wild Pitch

. . .

Eddie tried to see the reflection of the driver's face in his rearview mirror, but it was difficult. The trees along the road caused the sun to throw flickering shadows.

But then he recognized it and yelled, "It's her cousin!"

"Oh, no!" cried Tip. "What's he trying to do? Run you down?"

They were nearing an intersection. "Cut down here!" Eddie exclaimed, his voice high, tense.

That cousin of Monahan's must be sick, he thought. For Pete's sake, he wasn't really serious, was he? He wouldn't dare run me down, would he?

Eddie made the sharp turn to the right, pulling up close to the curb and then swinging up into the first driveway he came to. Tip followed him. They both stopped on the sidewalk and looked at the green coupe that had pursued them around the corner. It kept on going, but Eddie couldn't fail to see the dirty look on the face of the driver and his upheld fist.

"The guy's crazy!" he said, staring at the black smoke spewing from the exhaust pipe. "How long is he going to keep hounding me?"

"If he does it again, call the cops," Tip suggested. "I would."

"I'm going to."

They waited till the car was out of sight, then

coasted down the driveway and pedalled up the street.

Eddie realized that his breathing was faster than normal and that his palms were sweaty. The guy had scared him more than he thought.

9

Eddie waited until Monday to go to the hospital to see Phyllis Monahan. He thought that her friends and relatives would be visiting her over the weekend, and seeing her with them around was the last thing in the world he wanted.

He picked another batch of flowers and asked his mother to fix them so he could take them with him. She had caught a cold and decided to stay home that day. She trimmed the flowers and arranged them in an attractive bouquet.

"Nice job, Mom," Eddie said. "But how about wrapping paper around it?"

She smiled. "Why? So no one will see what you're carrying?"

He shrugged. "If Tip or Puffy saw me carrying flowers they'd know exactly whom I'm taking them to, and maybe get funny ideas."

"Like what?"

He grinned coyly.

"Like maybe I like her."

His mother smiled.

"Well, you are trying to make up to her, aren't you?"

That was true, of course. But it wasn't that he *liked* her. Liking her and trying to make up to her were two different things.

"I guess I am," he admitted.

"Then don't feel self-conscious about taking the flowers," she told him. "I think it's a beautiful gesture, no matter what your reasons are."

She got a roll of Saran wrap from under the kitchen sink, tore off a piece from it, and wrapped it around the flowers.

Eddie watched her, while her words ran through his mind again, and he wondered if he detected a double meaning in them. Frowning, he said, "Mom, you don't think that I . . . that I really like her, do you?"

Her eyes twinkled, and she grabbed him by the shoulders and turned him so that he faced the door. "So what's so terrible about it if you do?" she said. "Girls and boys don't have to be enemies forever just because of a wild pitch, do they?"

He pondered that as he headed toward the door, and agreed with her. But what was Monahan's opinion about that? If she was anything like that crazy cousin of hers, he might as well forget about ever getting on friendly terms with her.

He went out, looked up and down the street, saw no one he knew coming from either direction, and hurried to the garage. He opened the door, got out his bike, and rode it to the hospital.

As he stepped up to the receptionist, he saw by the large wall clock behind her that it was five minutes after two.

"Good afternoon," the woman greeted him sweetly. "Help you?"

"May I see Phyllis Monahan?"

The woman adjusted her pince-nez glasses and smiled. "I'm sorry, but only two people can see her at a time. There are two visiting her now, and two are waiting. Would you like to sit down and wait?"

He looked behind him and felt a sinking sensation in the pit of his stomach. One of the two people sitting in the waiting room was Monahan's cousin. Their eyes met, and Eddie thought he had never seen such a cold look in his life. With the cousin was a girl a few years younger than he. Probably his sister, Eddie guessed.

He turned back to the receptionist and hoped that his discomfort didn't show.

"I don't think I'll wait," he said.

"Suit yourself."

He looked at the flowers in his hand, conscious of their pleasant smell, and wondered whether to leave them. Sure as heck Monahan's relatives were eyeing him this very minute, wondering what he was going to do, too.

He looked back at the woman. "Thank you," he said, coming to a decision, and left.

Outside, he started down the steps and flung the flowers between two clumps of bushes. He would've left the flowers with the receptionist if that darn cousin of Monahan's hadn't been there.

I wonder what he would've said if I had left them? Eddie asked himself. Would he have demanded them from the receptionist and thrown them in the basket? Or would he have been more clever and told the receptionist politely that he'd take them up to Phyllis when he went to see her, and then thrown them away?

Whatever, Eddie felt better not leaving them. He went to the parking lot, got on his bike, and took off for home. His thoughts remained on Monahan. He wondered if he'd ever get to see her while she was in the hospital. Maybe he should have stayed, he thought.

And what about that ding-a-ling cousin of hers? I can't let him haunt me every time I see him. One of these days I've got to face him, because one of these days I'm going to see Monahan. I've got to. I'm not going to let her keep thinking that I hit her on purpose. All her friends probably think the same thing, and would make her believe it too. I have to fix that — fix it as soon as possible.

He got home and told his mother what he had done with the flowers.

She frowned at him. "You threw them away? Why, for Pete's sake?"

"Because her cousin was there," he said. "He doesn't like me. He thinks I hit Phyllis on purpose and wants to get even with me."

"Get *even* with you? What do you mean? How is he going to get even with you? You mean, beat you up?"

"I don't know. But he came up awfully close behind me with his car the other day while I was riding my bike on the street."

His mother stared at him. "Why did you wait until now to tell me that?"

"I didn't want to worry you," he said.

"But it's okay to worry me now."

"Oh, Mom," he said, stuck for anything more to say.

"Do you know his name?" she demanded. "Such terrible behavior should be reported to the police, and I've got a mind to do it."

"Forget it, Mom," he said calmly. "I think he was just trying to scare me. He wouldn't dare run me down."

She looked at him worriedly. "Suppose he does it again?"

He took hold of her hands. They felt cold and damp. "Take it easy, Mom. Okay? Don't worry. Once I see Monahan and explain things to her everything will be straightened out. I'm sure it will."

"But you've just been to the hospital, and you didn't go to see her," his mother said, looking him straight in the eye.

He went to the table and sat down, and remembered back a few years ago when she was in the hospital.

"Mom, I remember that Dad used to visit you sometimes in the mornings when you had your operation. Do you suppose I'd be able to see Monahan sometime in the morning, too?"

The concern slowly left her eyes. "It won't hurt to try."

He smiled, as if he'd just discovered an ace up his sleeve. "I'll go tomorrow morning," he said, enthusiastic. "Like you say, it won't hurt to try."

After breakfast the next morning he got to thinking about his proposed visit to Phyllis Monahan and decided against taking flowers to her. He was fed up picking flowers and then not being able to see her for one crazy reason or another. He would rather not take anything, just in case he wouldn't be able to see her again this time. But he felt that a gift, no matter how simple, would be good.

"I'm going to try to visit Phyllis Monahan in the hospital this morning, Rox," he said to his sister. "I hate to carry something in, but I feel I should. What do you think?"

They were in the kitchen, and she was putting fingernail polish on her nails.

"I think you should, too."

"Got any suggestions? And don't mention flowers. I've been batting zero with them."

She laughed. "Take her a box of chocolates. I know where you can get the best for less."

"Yeah. Me, too," he said. "Okay. That's a good idea. Thanks."

It was ten minutes of eleven when he rode his bike to his parents' gift shop and picked up a box of chocolates. His mother, who was working this morning, was easily convinced that the candy was for a good cause and therefore wouldn't charge him for it. (He knew she wouldn't have charged him even if he'd wanted it for himself, as long as he didn't make a habit of it.)

She wrapped it up for him, and he carried it to the hospital, arriving there at about ten after eleven.

The receptionist greeted him with a smile, and when he politely told her that he would like to see Miss Phyllis Monahan she politely informed him that he couldn't, because visiting hours were from two to four in the afternoons and seven to nine in the evenings.

His mouth sagged and he blinked a couple of times while he searched for words that might change her mind.

He looked down at the nicely wrapped box of chocolates in his hand and felt a tightening in his belly. What could he say to this sweet old lady anyway that could make her break that rule for just this one time? That he knew it was broken before? And that breaking it wasn't such a terrible infraction as she might want people to think?

He heard a soft voice and looked up to see the telephone operator leaning over to speak to the receptionist. A smile was on the telephone operator's face. Suddenly there was one on the receptionist's, too.

Then the telephone operator moved back and the receptionist focused her attention on Eddie. Her blue eyes twinkled behind her glasses.

"It's all right. You may go. She's in room three-fifteen."

"Thank you," said Eddie.

He flashed her a smile, then went through the open door and down the white-walled corridor that seemed a half a mile long. He was conscious of his heels clicking on the hard, vinyl floor and tried not to put all his weight on his heels.

He went around the corner, found the elevator, and took it to the third floor. He saw arrows on a wall indicating the room numbers, and turned down the corridor to his right. Phyllis Monahan's room was the eighth one down on the left-hand side.

Her door was open. He paused briefly on the threshold and looked in. She lay in bed, with a bandage on her head. She was looking up at some-thing on the wall opposite her, and from the sound Eddie assumed it was a television program.

He stood there, wondering whether to knock on the door or walk in and announce himself. He was nervous and tense. How was she going to react when she saw him?

Then he heard another voice — a woman's — and the bands in his stomach grew tighter.

Monahan had a visitor. Who was it? Her mother?

Why hadn't the receptionist said something about

her? Didn't she know? Well, maybe she didn't. It wasn't her business to know every visitor that entered the hospital.

Eddie took a step to the side and saw her. She was an older woman who didn't resemble Phyllis.

Suddenly their eyes met, and instant recognition flared in hers.

"Well!" she declared.

Eddie paled.

He saw Phyllis look away from the television set, glance momentarily at the woman, and shift her attention to him.

Her eyes widened.

"Eddie Rhodes?" she said. "Aren't you Eddie Rhodes?"

"Yes," he said.

10

He stepped into the room. It was warm and smelled faintly of disinfectant.

"How you doing?" he asked nervously.

She looked at him curiously, her eyes dropping briefly to the box he was holding.

"Fine. But I never thought I'd see you here. What've you got there?"

He smiled. "A present."

"A present for me? Or is it a flag of truce?"

"Maybe both," he said tensely, and handed it to her.

"Thank you. Oh, wow."

He forced a grin. "I was afraid you'd think I had hit you on purpose, and I didn't. It was a wild pitch. An accident."

She looked at the woman by the window.

"Mom, this is Eddie Rhodes," she said. "My mother, Eddie."

Eddie met the woman's eyes. They were brown, wide, and cold.

"I know," she replied stiffly before Eddie could speak. "I recognized him the minute he stepped into the room."

Her voice chilled him, and Eddie felt like turning around and walking out. But an inner voice compelled him to stay — at least for a little while longer.

"Hi, Mrs. Monahan," he said quietly.

"You're the one who almost ran into me with your bike," Phyllis broke in. "You, and another kid."

"Yes," he said, then frowned, slightly piqued. "Look, you don't think I did that on purpose, too, do you?"

She tightened her lips.

"I don't know. But you seem to cause the most peculiar accidents and they all happen to me."

He shook his head. "I know. But they *were* accidents. Especially hitting you on the head. I'm pretty wild at times. It's not the first time I've thrown a pitch like that."

"Then you shouldn't pitch!" Mrs. Monahan snapped angrily.

Both Eddie and Phyllis looked around at her. She had gotten off her chair, and was standing there; her eyes glittered.

"If you know you're a wild pitcher, you shouldn't be pitching. You should know better, and your coach should know better," she said hotly. "What if she hadn't been wearing that helmet? That ball might've killed her. You're lucky, young man, that it wasn't worse than it was, or I'd see to it that — "

"Mom, please," Phyllis interrupted.

Eddie's heart thumped like a machine. "I think I'll leave," he said, and started for the door.

"No, wait!" Phyllis called to him.

He paused and looked at her and saw her turn to her mother. "Mom, do you mind if . . . if we talked alone for a minute?" she asked calmly.

Mrs. Monahan frowned.

"What can you talk about?"

"Please, Mom?"

Her mother glared at her, then at Eddie. "This is ridiculous," she exclaimed, and stormed out of the room. He could hear her hard heels click against the tiled floor as she went down the corridor.

Phyllis motioned to him. "Come closer so we won't have to talk so loudly," she said.

He stepped up closer to the bed, feeling a sense of guilt because she had asked her mother to leave the room. He was nervous, and looked around at the flock of get-well cards scotch-taped to the wall behind her, and a stack of letters on the table beside her.

"You can't blame my mother," Phyllis said softly. "Both she and my dad were very worried about me. I was in a coma for a whole day, you know."

"All I know is that you were in intensive care for a couple of days."

She searched his eyes. "How did you know that?"

"I've been wanting to see you, but there was always someone here. That's why I came this morning."

"You mean it? You've been trying to see me?"

He nodded. "Would I lie about that?"

She shrugged her shoulders. "I don't know."

"Well, I wouldn't. I'm no jerk. And I mean it when I say I didn't hit you on purpose."

She closed her eyes and took a deep breath.

"Will you do me a favor?" she asked, opening her eyes again. "Will you crank up this end of the bed? There's a crank there on the end."

"Sure."

He found the crank, wound it a few times, and got her up to where she sat comfortably.

"Thanks," she said. She looked at the box. "You didn't have to do this, you know."

"I know, but I wanted to."

"What a beautiful wrapping job!"

"My mother did it."

"I hate to ruin it. But — do you mind?"

"No. I'd like you to. If you don't like what's in it, I'll take it home and eat it myself."

"Candy!" she said, tearing off the wrapper. "Chocolates?"

"Right. Worst thing for teeth you can eat."

"Hmmmm!" she smiled, delighted.

Once she had the outside wrapper off she tore off the cellophane wrapper, then opened the box. "Oh, wow!" she cried. "Yummyyummyyummy! Can I sample one now?"

"They're yours. Sample them all if you want to. No. Better not. Save some for your mother."

She smiled at him, then picked out a chocolate-coated cherry and bit off half of it.

Eddie watched her, feeling good that he had brought her a gift she appreciated. Thank you, Roxie.

"What about your head?" he asked, looking at the bandage she had wrapped around it. "How soon can you play baseball again? Did the doctor say?"

She looked at the other piece of the chocolate. "He said it might be a long time. It was quite a bang, you know."

"Yes, I know." He watched her plunk the piece into her mouth and start chewing it. "Did he say you would be able to play again this year?"

"I didn't ask him."

"Why not?"

"I was afraid to."

He frowned. "Because he might say you shouldn't?"

She searched for another piece of candy, then suddenly held out the box to him.

"Boy, am I dumb. I guess I left my manners home. Here, take one."

"No, thanks." He was anxious to know more about her condition, how serious the injury was. "Are you afraid he might say you shouldn't?"

"I guess so."

He went over to the wall and read a few of the cards. Some were serious, some humorous. One large card with a picture of a sick dog holding a thermometer in its mouth was signed "Love, from Mingo."

Eddie looked at Phyllis. "Mingo? Is that Chinese?"

She laughed. "No! That's his name. He's my cousin."

Eddie frowned. "A big kid? Dark hair? Kind of wild?"

"That could be him. You know him?"

"Know him? He's been after me ever since I hit you. I thought he was going to run me down with his car the other day. You sure he's not a case for the guys in the white coats?"

She smiled. "He told me he was going to get you

one of these days, but I told him to lay off. He hasn't bothered you any more, has he?"

"No. But I thought that's because he hasn't seen me on the streets. I saw him here in the lounge yesterday. Him and a girl."

She frowned at him. "You were here yesterday?"

He nodded.

"Why didn't you come to see me? Did he scare you away?"

He chuckled wryly. "Well, when I saw him and the girl sitting there, I knew they were waiting for somebody to come back from seeing you so they'd be able to go. I didn't think I had a chance, so I left."

"That was Sally, his girl friend. They didn't tell me they saw you."

"I figured that when you didn't mention it earlier."

She shook her head disgustedly. "Mingo acts as though he's my older brother sometimes. He's even forbidden me to see certain movies after he's seen them. My parents think that's all right, but I think I've reached the age to make up my own mind about such matters. How about you?"

Eddie shrugged. "Tip and I — you know Tip."

"Yes. Your friend."

"Right. He and I see a couple of movies a month. Those that kids our age can see. Action pictures mostly."

"I love them, too," she said.

She ate another chocolate, then closed the box and set it on the table.

"Those were delicious," she said, beaming. "Did I say thanks? If not — thanks."

"You're welcome." He took a deep breath and let it out. "Well, I'm really glad I came this morning."

She tilted her head. "I am, too. I was afraid you'd be the type of guy I'd hate for the rest of my life."

"I was afraid of that. That's why I came."

She looked deeply into his eyes.

"How old are you?"

"Fourteen."

"So am I."

"You look older."

"I know. That's why my dad wanted me to be a first baseman."

His forehead creased. "Was it his idea that you play baseball?"

She shook her head.

"No. It was mine. I've played ever since I could lift a bat. Dad was a baseball player, and I'm an only child, so as I grew older we played together an awful lot. Lately, though, he hasn't had much time. He's got a different job."

She shrugged, as if she didn't care about pursuing the topic.

Wild Pitch

. . .

Eddie looked at her, suddenly glad he had made it a point to see her, to know her better. She wasn't a jerk kid, a girl who just happened to be a good baseball player, he thought. She was intelligent, and understanding. In spite of how he had felt about a girl playing on a baseball team before, he thought she deserved another break. It was his duty to give it to her.

"In that case, maybe I can help you," he said.

She folded her hands on her lap and looked at him. "What do you mean?"

"I'd like to help you get back to playing baseball."

She looked at him, opened her mouth as if to say something, but remained silent as footsteps sounded just outside the door.

Eddie turned and saw Mrs. Monahan in the doorway.

"May I come in now?" she asked with a hard edge to her voice.

Both Eddie and her daughter looked at her.

"Yes, Mom," said Phyllis, and pursed her lips.

"I've got to go," said Eddie. "Maybe next time I'll see you in the afternoon."

He headed for the door, and paused briefly in front of Mrs. Monahan.

"It was nice meeting you, Mrs. Monahan," he said, and walked out.

11

Eddie was at the hospital at twenty minutes of two the next afternoon in order to be the first one in to see Phyllis. He expected her mother to be one of the earlier visitors, and wondered what she'd say to him if she arrived after he did and saw him waiting in the lobby.

As it turned out it was Phyllis's cousin, Mingo, who showed up at five minutes of two. Eddie, sitting in the lobby, saw the tall, dark-haired youth come in and walk directly to the desk. His girl friend was with him. She turned briefly, looked directly at him, then turned back to Mingo.

Eddie saw him speak to the receptionist, then saw her give him two cards.

They started to head for the corridor, but then he saw the girl say something to Mingo, and saw them both glance back over their shoulders at him.

The dark, annoyed burn in Mingo's eyes was unmistakable.

They turned away and walked on.

How do you like that? Eddie thought, turning to glare at the receptionist. I thought visiting hours were *strictly* from two to four!

Bull!

He didn't know whether to continue waiting or not, but decided he would. Maybe Mingo and his girl friend would not stay too long. If they left early, and Mrs. Monahan didn't show up, he could spend a few minutes with Phyllis. Maybemaybemaybe.

Mrs. Monahan came in at ten after two. She had hardly stepped into the lobby when she glanced toward the seats and saw him.

"Hi, Mrs. Monahan," he greeted her quietly.

Her lips formed the word "Hello" before she turned away from him.

She paused briefly at the desk, then went on through the corridor.

Eddie looked at the gray-haired head of the receptionist. What kind of deal was this, anyway? he wondered.

He got up and walked to the desk. The gray head lifted. Her nice, mature face smiled. "Yes? Oh, hello, there."

"Hi. I just saw three people go in to visit Miss Monahan. I thought that only" — a nervous feeling crept up and he had to swallow—"that only two people were allowed to see her at a time."

The smile broadened.

"That's right. But the third person was Mrs. Monahan, Miss Monahan's mother. We don't keep mothers or fathers waiting to see their children. Now, as soon as one or both of the others comes back—"

"Okay. I'll wait," Eddie cut in, knowing what she was going to say. He started back to his seat.

"Will you let me have your name, please?" she called to him. "As soon as a card's available, I'll call you."

"Eddie Rhodes," he said.

"Thank you."

It was nearly two-thirty when Mingo and the girl returned from visiting Phyllis. They handed their cards back to the receptionist, then Mingo turned and focused his attention on Eddie. He left the girl and came forward, a cold, disturbed look on his face.

"You here to see Phyl?"

Eddie returned his gaze. "Yes."

"Why?"

Eddie started to answer when the receptionist

called his name. He excused himself, got a card from her, then came back to Mingo.

"Because I want to help her get back into baseball," he said bluntly. "I feel I owe her that much."

Mingo stared at him. "You mean you want to help her after what you did to her? I don't believe it."

"I don't care if you do or not. But it's true. Excuse me."

He started toward the corridor, and Mingo grabbed his arm.

"Rhodes, you're in for a big, fat surprise."

Eddie searched the dark eyes. "What do you mean?"

"She doesn't want to play anymore. She's through. Finished. Thanks to you, pal."

Eddie's hopes took a plunge. "I don't believe you."

Mingo's eyes glittered. "You don't have to. She'll tell you that personally."

"See ya," Eddie said.

He turned and walked down the long corridor, feeling surprised and hurt by what Mingo had told him. He took the elevator to Phyllis's room and found her sitting up in bed with her mother sitting on a chair close by her. They exchanged greetings, then Mrs. Monahan got up and stepped out of the room, saying she'd be back in ten minutes.

"I suppose that means I should be out of here by the end of that time," Eddie said softly to Phyllis, smiling.

"Not necessarily."

She had one hand on her lap, the other combing her hair. "Been waiting long?"

"Since twenty minutes of two."

She frowned. "Twenty minutes of two?"

"Yeah. But that's okay. I finally made it. Feeling better?"

"Much better. I'd like to get out of here right now."

"What's the rush? Aren't they treating you right?"

"Oh, sure. It's not that. The nurses are great, except for the one who comes in early in the morning, wakes me up, and hands me a pill. It's just that I can't do anything. All I do is sleep, eat, and take pills. It's driving me up a wall."

Eddie grinned. "How about baseball?"

"What about it?"

"Are you anxious to get started again?"

He didn't want to tell her what Mingo had said about her decision to quit. Not yet, anyway.

She stopped combing her hair, laid the comb on top of the table, and looked at him.

"Why? Why should you care?"

"Why shouldn't I care? It's my fault you're in here, isn't it?"

"You said it was an accident."

"Sure, it was. But it's still my fault. So I feel I owe you one."

"You owe me nothing."

He went to the window, wondering whether he'd be able to cope with her. He turned back to her. "I'll help you play again, Phyl," he said seriously.

She met his eyes.

"In a pig's eye you will."

He stared at her. "You don't want me to?"

"Do you think that just because I'm a girl I can't do it without your help? I worked myself up to playing on a boys' team, and I think I did a good job at first base until you threw that clunker. I think I can make a comeback on my own" — she paused, looking away from him — "if I make a comeback at all."

Now it comes, he thought.

"What do you mean 'if'?" he asked.

She shrugged and studied her nails. "I've decided not to play anymore."

Eddie stood, slightly stunned. He thought he'd be prepared for it, but hearing it from her own lips affected him more than he had expected it would.

He came away from the window, stood by the bed,

and looked at her. She kept studying her nails; an excuse, he suspected, for her to keep from meeting his eyes.

"You can't quit, Phyl," he told her.

Her eyes popped up. "Oh, can't I? Who said so? You?"

"Yes. You'd be giving up. Not only that, but you'd be letting your mother and father down. They wanted you to play."

"Now you sound like a father. Or a shrink. Are you going to major in psychiatry when you go to college?" she asked smartly.

He grinned. "Quit kidding, Phyl. Be serious."

Her eyes filled with tears. "I — I'm just afraid that I — I can't face a pitcher anymore!"

"Any pitcher? Or just me?"

"I don't know!"

Their eyes met and held. Then she looked away, grabbed a tissue from the table, and wiped her eyes.

"That's the biggest reason why you can't quit, Phyl," Eddie said. "You've *got* to get back into baseball. Don't you see? You've got to get over that feeling. And I want to help you. I mean it. I really want to help you."

Her eyes reddened.

"I'll — I'll think about it," she said.

He smiled. "I hope you will. I'm going now. Your mother should be coming back soon, anyway." He headed for the door. "Take care."

"I will. Thanks for coming, Eddie."

12

There was a game on Wednesday. The Lancers were up against the Bruins, and Eddie had to pitch because Harry was sick.

Eddie looked at the coach, pleased for the chance to pitch again, but suddenly worried, too, that he might throw another wild pitch and hit another batter.

The coach seemed to have read his thoughts as he patted Eddie on the shoulder and said, "We have only two guys on our pitching staff, Eddie, ol' boy. You've *got* to pitch. I could put Larry, or Paul, or any of the other guys in there, but I don't want this game turned into a circus. The Bruins are good, and you're the only one I've got who can pitch against them and make this a ball game. Okay?"

Eddie shrugged. He wasn't going to argue. He didn't believe in questioning a coach's decision, even if he disagreed with it. Anyway, he knew he couldn't have changed the coach's mind, so why argue?

"What have you heard about Phyllis Monahan?" Coach Inger asked him.

"She's coming along okay."

"Good. Have you been up to see her?"

"Yes."

"I'm going up tonight," said the coach. "Okay, Eddie. Try to keep the ball in there. Don't throw too hard, just try to concentrate on the plate." He grinned placidly. "Don't worry about a thing."

Oh, sure. Don't worry about a thing. Why did coaches say that when worry was part of the game? Eddie shrugged, then dismissed the thought.

The Bruins had first bats, and Eddie walked up to the mound as if he were a stranger to it. His palms were sweaty. He scooped up a handful of soft dirt, rubbed it over his palms, then dropped it at his feet.

The ump handed a new ball to Tip, and Tip tossed it to him. Eddie threw in a half dozen pitches, trying to hit Tip's target with each one, and succeeded four out of six times.

"Play ball!" said the ump, then turned his back to Eddie and wiped off the plate with a whisk broom.

The Bruins' leadoff batter stepped to the plate, and Eddie sized him up. He was short, heavy, and held his bat high over his right shoulder.

"Nothing too good, Eddie, boy!" Larry called from third.

Wild Pitch

· · ·

"No sticker! No sticker, Eddie!" Puffy's voice boomed from short.

From Tony in right field: "Juice it by 'im, Eddie! Juice it by 'im!"

Somebody from the stands yelled, "Don't hit him, Eddie!"

Somebody else yelled, "This one's a he, Eddie! Be good to him!"

Laughter followed the yells.

Eddie reddened as he toed the rubber and looked at the ball, turning it so that his first two fingers crossed the laces. He pretended he wasn't listening to the needling remarks, but the voices were so clear coming from behind third base he couldn't miss them.

He walked the man on five pitches, then tried to take it easier on the second batter, expecting him to bunt. Instead, the batter laced the ball out to right center for two bases, and a run scored.

Tip and Puffy came in toward the mound and tried to settle him down.

"Don't listen to those monkeys in the stands," said Puffy. "They don't know any better."

"This next batter's big, but he swings like an old, rusty gate," said Tip, spitting into his mitt. "Throw 'em fast and you'll whiff 'im."

Wild Pitch
. . .

Eddie wasn't worried about throwing them fast; he was worried about hitting a batter. His second pitch almost nicked the big kid's belt, but he hit the corners on the next two, then struck the kid out.

"There you go, Eddie!" Tip yelled, laughing.

A pop fly to Puffy and a grounder to Paul at second base ended the top of the first inning.

Eddie walked off the mound amid a chorus of cheers from Lancer fans.

"See, Eddie? You did all right," Coach Inger said, tapping him on the back. "Your control looks pretty good."

Eddie shrugged. Must be that my nervousness wasn't showing, he thought.

The Lancers picked up two runs on Larry's walk, Lynn's double to left center, and Tip's single over first.

The Bruins scored in the top of the second on a walk and two singles. One of Eddie's pitches soared over Tip's leaping reach, and another moved the batter back six inches, drawing jeers from the fans.

"Keep them *away* from the batter," Tip advised him as they walked off the field together. "Most of your pitches seem to be on the batter's side. No wonder the crowd thinks you're trying to brush him off sometimes."

"I don't. I never do."

"I know that," exclaimed Tip. "But the fans don't."

When the Lancers finally got up again, Puffy led off with a single. Eddie got Coach Inger's sign to bunt, but after two foul tips he had to swing or risk a strikeout. He swung, and belted a single over shortstop. Puffy ran to second and tried to stretch it to third, only to get tagged out trying a Pete Rose slide on his belly.

Larry got on again, this time on an error by the shortstop, who made a nice catch of Larry's grounder, then heaved it a mile over the first baseman's head.

Two singles in a row by Dale and Lynn helped the Lancers put two more runs on the board. Bruins 2, Lancers 4.

Eddie walked the first batter in the top of the third. The second Bruin laid down a bunt to move up the runner, but the ball only bounced two feet in front of the plate. Tip pounced on it like a cat and threw out the runner at second. Puffy, making the play, almost doubled the runner at first, but missed by a step.

"Nice going, Tip," said Eddie.

Sometimes Tip could pull a move that would surprise everybody.

No Bruin scored that inning, and the Lancers

came up with hopes to gain on them, or go ahead. They did neither.

It wasn't till the fourth inning that Eddie laid in a strike on the leadoff batter. Then he threw one that got away from him. It was so far inside that even though the batter jumped back the ball grazed his thigh.

The ump pointed a finger toward first base. The batter, tossing aside his bat, glared at Eddie, rubbed his side, and trotted to first.

Eddie heard the crowd taunting him. He tried hard to ignore them, but couldn't.

He walked the next batter, then eased up on a pitch on the third, heard the solid sound of bat connecting with ball, and watched in awe as it soared over the left-field fence for a home run.

He stayed in there, mentally pleading for Mr. Inger to yank him. Finally, Mr. Inger did.

A mixture of jeers and applause saluted him as he walked off the mound, and his throat choked.

"Chin up, Eddie," encouraged Tip. "You pitched a good game."

Eddie knew better. If that was a good one, I'd hate to pitch a bad one, he thought. But Tip seemed to know what bothered him, seemed to know when to apply a comforting word, and Eddie appreciated his try.

Wild Pitch

· · ·

Coach Inger had Don Tanglefoot, the substitute infielder, warm up in the bullpen. When he yanked Eddie out he waved Don in. After a half dozen throws — some looked strong, some weak — Don was ready.

The Bruins scored another run before Don pulled the Lancers out from under the onslaught. The Bruins scored a run in the sixth, and Puffy powdered a home run in the bottom of the sixth. After seven innings it was Bruins 7, Lancers 5.

Eddie had little to say as he walked home with Tip, Puffy, and Margie. His mind was wrapped up in his poor performance and the fear of hitting another batter. Good thing there were helmets, he thought. He'd have batters scared to death of his pitching.

He wondered if he'd ever improve. Speed, control, and something on the ball were all that a pitcher needed. Well, he had speed, and sometimes control, and sometimes he could make the ball do funny things. He always felt good when the ball cooperated, and lousy when it didn't.

Tip, Puffy, and Margie carried the conversation. Tip didn't think the Bruins should've won. If Tony hadn't been half asleep on that hit to short right field, he would've taken off in time and caught the ball instead of grabbing it on a hop and letting a run score. If this and if that. Eddie felt awful.

He and Margie got home and found Roxie ready to leave for the gift shop to relieve their parents. She asked about the game and he said he didn't think she'd care to hear about it.

"Lousy, huh?" she said.

"Lousy's right," he answered.

"You didn't hit anybody again, did you?"

"I did."

Her eyes flashed to Margie and back to him. "You did?"

"He did," Margie cut in, nodding.

"Eddie! Maybe you should give up pitching," Roxie declared. "Out of nine positions on the field you should be able to play another one."

"It seems so, doesn't it?"

She looked surprised. "You mean you can't play another position? Just pitch?"

He shrugged. "Well, I've tried to play shortstop, but I'm lousy on grounders. I can also throw a ball pretty far over the first baseman's head. That's why Puffy Garfield's playing shortstop and not me."

"What about the outfield?"

"I've worked out there, too. I might as well buck for a mascot's job."

Roxie looked at her watch. "I've got to run, or Mom and Dad will fire me."

"What's to eat?"

"I had cottage cheese and peaches," Roxie replied, opening the door. "If you don't think that will fill you, wait for Mom. She'll fix you kids something. Take care. Oh — are you going to see Phyllis tonight?"

"I think so."

She smiled. "Good. 'Bye, now."

" 'Bye."

At five of seven he rode his bike to the hospital, remembering that Coach Inger had said he was going to visit Phyllis, too. He was full. His mother had cooked chicken and rice, and he had eaten like a horse.

He stepped up to the counter, saw the same gray hair, the same face, the same pleasant smile.

"She left this morning," the receptionist said, before he had a chance to say a word.

He frowned, surprised. "Oh? Thank you."

13

Eddie felt a sense of relief. If she was sent home she must be lots better, he thought.

He wondered if Coach Inger had been here yet, but he turned and left without inquiring.

As he rode out of the parking lot, he decided he'd head for her home.

He rode directly there, parked in the driveway next to a blue car, climbed the steps to the front porch, and thumbed the door bell. Somewhere in the house, chimes rang. Presently the door opened and a tall, broad-shouldered man in shirtsleeves stood there.

"Yes?"

"Hi," Eddie said nervously. "I'm Eddie Rhodes. I went to the hospital to see Phyl, but the lady told me she came home."

"Yes, she did. I'm Phyllis's father. Come in."

"Thanks."

Mr. Monahan led him through the house, a large

home with a thick yellow rug through the hall and the rooms, landscape reproductions on the walls, and pastel furniture. Phyl and her mother were sitting on comfortable lawn chairs on the porch.

Phyl's eyes widened in surprise when she saw him. "Eddie!"

"Hi," he said calmly. "Hello, Mrs. Monahan." He went over and shook her hand.

"Well, hello," she greeted him politely. "Were you at the hospital?"

"Yes."

She started to get up.

"No, please," he said. "Don't get up."

She smiled. "This is Mr. Monahan," she said.

"I met him," Eddie said, smiling. They shook hands.

"So you're Eddie Rhodes, huh?" said Mr. Monahan, crossing his arms over his chest and looking at Eddie from his six-foot-two height. "I'm glad to meet you finally."

Eddie blushed.

"Sit down, Eddie," Mrs. Monahan offered.

He sat in one of the other chairs and looked at Phyllis. Her face was radiant, although she had lost some of her tan. Her hair was cut to shoulder length. She wasn't wearing a bandage anymore.

"Did you have a ball game today?" she asked.

"Yes. Against the Bruins. We lost."

He didn't want to talk baseball, not in front of the Monahans. But Phyl kept asking questions.

"Did you pitch?"

He nodded. "Four innings."

She frowned. "Just four?"

"Yeah. I was being blasted."

He looked at his hands. He felt awkward and uncomfortable. He got up.

"Well," he said, "I just wanted to — "

"Why don't you two walk around the backyard a bit," Mr. Monahan interrupted. "The doctor says you should start walking a little more, Phyl. Build up those loose muscles."

"Good idea!" she exclaimed.

They stepped down from the porch to the yard, where clusters of hibiscus and petunias waved in the breeze.

"Your mother's attitude toward me seems to have changed," Eddie observed quietly.

"Oh, it was only for a short while that she thought you were such an ogre. It didn't last long. As a matter of fact, Mom and Dad were discussing you a little while ago."

"They were?"

109

"They wondered if you'd come to the house."

He grinned.

"How about that?"

Now that they were alone, he brought up the subject of baseball. The last time he'd seen her she was considering quitting, and he had pleaded with her to give herself another chance.

"Well, I hope you've decided to keep playing, Phyl," he said, watching her face, looking for a reaction.

"I've decided," she said.

"To do what?" he asked when she didn't tell him immediately.

"To play," she replied, and laughed.

His heart jumped. He felt like throwing his arms around her. "Oh, good, Phyl! I'm so glad!"

"I thought you'd be," she told him.

He stayed for fifteen minutes, talking baseball, and about working out with her as soon as her doctor said she could. She beamed with enthusiasm.

"I can hardly wait, Eddie!" she cried.

Harry started to pitch against the Pirates on Tuesday, but after they knocked six runs off him in the first two innings, Coach Inger had Eddie go in and sent Harry to the showers.

Eddie concentrated on control, hitting the pocket of Tip's mitt wherever Tip held it. He threw hard, and most of the time accurately. Slightly inside of the plate, slightly outside, now and then low or high, depending on where Tip wanted the ball pitched. He threw only a few curves, conceding that his weren't that effective, anyway.

The Pirates scored one run off him in the fourth, two in the fifth, and two in the sixth. He walked four men. Don Tanglefoot relieved him.

The Pirates took the game, 11 to 3.

He got a warm surprise when he started to walk off the field. Someone was calling his name, and he recognized the voice immediately.

His heart thumped as he turned and saw Phyllis running across the grass toward him.

"Not too fast!" he yelled at her. "Not too fast!"

She came up to him, breathing hard, laughing. "What a game!" she declared.

"I know. It stunk. And so did I."

"Not as much as that first kid did."

"That was Harry, and he's our regular."

"Too bad."

"Hey, meet my sister, Margie. And this is Puffy and Tip."

"Glad to meet you," Margie said.

"Same here," said Puffy and Tip.

"Hi," she said, and wiped the sweat off her forehead. "Boy, it's hot. Well, I've got to be going. See you all."

She took off.

"Hey, she's okay," said Margie.

"Ditto," said Puffy.

"Ditto," echoed Tip.

Eddie telephoned her after he got through supper and asked her if she'd like to play catch with him.

"You bet!" she told him. "But I'm still eating. Be here about twenty of."

He was there on the dot with his glove. She had a baseball — four or five of them, she said — and they played catch. They had plenty of room, a big yard with a metal fence around it.

He came over the next afternoon again, and they played more catch. She had a bat — three or four of them, too — and they played pepper. He hit them to her first, lightly, so that she wouldn't exert herself. Then she hit them to him. He saw when she was tired, and they quit.

It rained the next morning, and he was afraid that the ground might be too wet for the Lancers–Bucs game. But the clouds cleared away by one o'clock, the sun came out, and by three o'clock the field was dry.

Wild Pitch
. . .

Puffy sat with him as the game started. The Lancers were batting.

"Heard you're spending a lot of time with Monahan," Puffy said.

"Maybe I am."

"You like her?"

Eddie shrugged. "She's okay."

Puffy shook his head. "I can't figure it out. She's all right now, isn't she? I mean, she got out of that hit on the head with no aftereffects. Why do you feel you owe her something?"

Eddie felt his skin prickle.

"I hit her. It was a wild pitch, an accident, but I threw the ball. So it was my fault. How many times do I have to say it?"

"But it could've been anybody. Suppose it was a guy — a male you had hit? What would you have done then?"

"If he told me he wasn't going to play baseball again, I'd probably do the same thing."

Puffy looked at him, his eyebrows arched. "That's what she told you? That she didn't want to play again?"

"Right."

"In that case — "

"Now you understand, I hope," Eddie cut in.

"I understand," Puffy replied quietly.

Wild Pitch

· · ·

The game was close all the way, and Harry pitched all seven innings of it. The Lancers won, 5–4.

Eddie and Phyl started to play more pepper, and more catch. They'd go to the ball diamond during the mornings when it was available and he'd knock out pop flies and grounders to her. She was leery of the grounders at first, but gradually she shed her fear of them and began to field them like a veteran.

"How about batting?" he asked her.

She blinked her eyes. "I don't know," she said reluctantly.

"I've brought a helmet," he said. He got it from his bike and tossed it to her. "Put it on."

She put it on and stepped alongside the bare spot on the ground five or six feet in front of the backstop screen. Eddie got within pitching distance of her, aimed at a spot in the screen directly over the bare spot on the ground, and pitched. He threw easily, cautiously, arching the ball, so that she'd have plenty of time to jump clear if it came at her.

The throw was good and she swung at it. She ticked it.

"You're swinging too hard," said Eddie.

She took it easier on the next pitch, which was in there, too, and drove it on the ground to short. He had three more balls, and she hit them all.

"This is crazy," she called to him as he turned and ran to the outfield after them.

It was, but if they wanted to continue practicing, he had to chase after them.

After the second time, a couple of kids rode up on their bikes. When they saw Eddie chasing the hit balls they left their bikes and chased after the balls themselves.

"Thanks, guys!" said Eddie appreciatively. "Be around again tomorrow, will you?"

"Maybe!" one of them answered.

But they were there the next day, and the next, and Eddie noticed a gradual improvement in Phyllis's batting. Most of all, she wasn't afraid of his pitches anymore. That was his ultimate goal.

14

He came down with a cold and didn't see her for a week. But she called him on the phone every day at about eleven o'clock and asked him how he was doing. He found himself waiting expectantly for it.

"You two have become pretty chummy," observed his mother. "How long is this going to last?"

"It's almost over," he told her.

Her eyebrows shot up in surprise. "Just like that?"

He shrugged. "She's all right now. She's able to play."

"The doctor say that?"

"Yes."

"I was wondering," she said.

It was the first part of August, and baseball season was drawing to a close. Phyllis called him one morning when he was better and asked him if he was well enough to go swimming in the gulf. He said he was, and he rode his bike to her place. They walked to the beach, a quarter of a mile away.

The water was warm, beautiful. They swam for two hours. He was so absorbed in having fun that when he suddenly remembered that the Lancers were scheduled to play the Bruins that afternoon, he almost panicked.

"Oh, man!" he cried, trudging out of the water and toweling himself quickly. "Where's my head? We've got a game this afternoon!"

She looked at him, beads of salt water dripping down her face. "Eddie?"

"Yeah?"

She grabbed up her towel and started rubbing it gently over her hair, which had grown a little longer since the last time he had seen her.

"You know it's almost over."

"Yes, I know."

"What're we going to do? I mean, we're not going to quit seeing each other, are we?"

"Of course not! Chances are we'll be playing against each other again next year. And maybe we can get together a few times before then. Okay?"

She nodded, and smiled. "You've been great to me. I just wanted to know where we stood."

He grinned.

"Wait'll we face each other in a ball game," he said.

Her eyes twinkled. She draped the towel over her shoulders.

"Would you try to strike me out?" she asked.

He laughed. "You're darn right I would. You think I'd let you try to knock the ball out of the lot on me? No way!"

They laughed together. He wrapped the towel around his hips and they hurried home.

The game was ready to start when he got there. The stands were packed. A chorus of cheers went up from the fans as he ran in from the gate to the Lancers' dugout.

"Well, look who's here," Puffy declared. "Who said he'd forgotten us?"

Coach Inger tossed him a ball. "Warm up, Eddie. I'll have Harry go the first two innings and put you in the last five."

He warmed up, throwing in the bullpen to Pete Turner, whose poor hitting kept his playing to a minimum. Coach Inger had a rule to play all of his men in every game, but not more than two or three innings if they weren't playing to his satisfaction.

The Lancers had first bats, and Eddie took a glance toward the field now and then to see how the guys were making out. Rod Bellow was the only one who got on, driving a single through the pitcher's box. He died there on first, though, as both Dale and Lynn flied out to the outfield.

Harry walked the first Bruin, but a double play and Puffy's neat catch of a line drive kept them from scoring.

Paul led off the action in the second inning with a single through the pitcher's box, then advanced to second base on Tip's sacrifice bunt.

"Keep it moving! Keep it moving!" Tony Netro kept shouting from the first-base coaching box. Eddie figured that Tony'd be playing the last few innings of the game, since Tom Hooker was starting at right field.

Tom clobbered a single over short, driving in Paul for the Lancers' first run, and Eddie felt a small sense of security. Even a one-run lead was better than no lead at all.

He waited for Puffy to bat before throwing again to Pete.

"Lay it out of the lot, Puff!" he yelled. The more runs now, the better.

Puffy connected with a double down the third-base line, driving Tom around the bases as if a swarm of bees were after him. The play at home was close. Harry, standing by, yelled for Tom to hit the dirt, and Tom did, sliding across the plate under the throw and the catcher's delayed tag.

"Safe!" the ump boomed.

Eddie, turning to continue his throws to Pete, smiled. He hoped the guys would keep up their hitting while he was on the mound. He'd probably need it.

He didn't watch Harry bat, but when he heard a yell he looked toward the diamond and saw a cloud of dust around third base, and the base umpire crouched over a prostrate Puffy Garfield, thumb sticking up into the air. Apparently Puffy had tried to steal and failed.

"The jerk," Pete said. "Why'd he run? He was in position to score."

Eddie shrugged. "Don't ask me. Ask Mr. Inger."

"I think he's bawling Puffy out," said Pete, glancing toward the field.

Eddie looked there and saw the coach hovering over Puffy, gesturing with his left hand in the direction of second base.

Eddie smiled. "I guess it was Puffy's idea to steal," he reflected. "Not Mr. Inger's."

The Bruins picked up a run at their turn at bat, but the Lancers got it back in the top of the third with a double off Dale's bat and a triple off Lynn's. Lancers 3, Bruins 1.

"Okay, Eddie, get in there," said Coach Inger. "How's his control, Pete?"

"Great."

"Good. Harry, take Lynn's place in center field."

Tip, buckling on his catcher's gear, looked at the coach in surprise. "Let's hope no balls are hit to him," he quipped.

The guys laughed.

Eddie, and everyone else on the team, knew that Harry's skill as an outfielder left a lot to be desired. Obviously the only reason the coach was keeping him in the game was for him to come to the team's rescue in case Eddie's pitching was dragging them under.

Eddie faced the first batter with mustered confidence, concentrating on each pitch in an effort to put it where Tip held his mitt. A couple were on target. A couple weren't.

"Watch him, Dave!" yelled a Bruin fan. "He can be wild!"

"Don't let him send you to the hospital!" yelled another.

Eddie tensed. The remarks stung.

He pitched, and the batter laced it down to third. Larry grabbed the low-bouncing ball, took a step, and whipped it to first for the out.

Eddie was careful with the next batter, a short, stubby-legged kid, and tried to keep the ball low and outside.

Each pitch was too low. Eddie walked him.

Tip ran out to the mound. "Hey, what're you doing? Can't you see my target?"

"I can see it," said Eddie glumly.

"Well, put it there. And, look. Quit listening to those jerks. You're not going to hit anybody."

"I sure don't want to."

Tip spat into his glove. "Let's get 'em."

He ran back to his position, and Eddie toed the rubber. He pitched well, and got the man out.

Tip gave him the V-for-victory sign as he headed for the dugout. "You're in the groove, Eddie. Just listen to your ol' buddy. That's all you've got to do, kid."

He thought he heard a familiar voice calling his name from the grandstand behind home plate. He looked up. Sure enough, it was Phyllis. She waved to him. He grinned and nodded, and glanced at the persons beside her. Two were girls he had seen visiting her at the hospital. The other was Mingo, her cousin. The expression on his face was somber.

Did he always have to be with her? What was he — her bodyguard?

He reached the bench, and squeezed in between Puffy and Harry.

"She up there in the stands?" asked Puffy.

Eddie nodded.

"How's she doing?"

"Okay."

"Just okay?"

"No. Better than okay. She can catch and throw and hit pretty good. She exercises quite a lot besides."

Harry nudged his arm, smiling. "You haven't fallen for her, have you?"

Eddie saw the elfin look in his eyes. "No, I haven't fallen for her."

"You sure? I heard my brother, Dick, tell my parents once that he wasn't sure he'd fallen for his girl until she went out west for a month to visit relatives."

"Your brother Dick's a lot older than I am."

"And dumber, too, I hope. Dick and that chick of his have more fights than a couple of roosters." He tapped Eddie's knee. "Hey, man, you're doing okay in there. Just don't do too good. I don't want to lose my job."

Eddie nudged him in the ribs. "Don't worry. I don't think you will. Why do you think Mr. Inger's kept you in the game?"

Harry's eyebrows shot up. "Why? Because he can count on my hitting?"

Both Eddie and Puffy laughed. "Clown!" snorted Puffy.

A figure blocked out the sun in front of Puffy.

"Puffy, we don't have a DH in this league," said Coach Inger, looking at him. "How about getting off that bench and picking up a club?"

The chunky shortstop looked at him in surprise. "Yeah!"

"You follow him, Harry," said the coach. "Shake a leg."

Both boys sprang off the bench and selected clubs from the bat rack. At the plate Tip swung at a chest-high pitch and drilled it to left center field for two bases.

It took Harry's surprising triple to drive him in. Then Harry himself scored on Larry's Texas-league hit over second.

Rod's strikeout ended the top half of the inning.

Eddie found it easier going back to the mound. He didn't feel completely at ease, but he wasn't as scared as he was earlier. He threw harder, and his average in putting the ball on target improved.

The Bruins got a hit off him, and their cleanup hitter blasted a home run over the right-field fence.

"Settle down, Eddie!" Tip yelled to him. "Don't work too fast!"

A wild pitch on the next batter drew a yell from the crowd. He wasn't proud when he struck out the batter. He walked off the field with his head bent in dejection, his eyes focused on the ground.

The Bruins held the Lancers scoreless in the top of the fifth, then picked up two themselves. In the top of the sixth, Puffy's double, Larry's single, Rod's triple, and Dale's single put the Lancers in the lead, 8 to 5.

The Bruins scored again in the bottom of the sixth, but failed to get a man on in the seventh. The Lancers won, 8–6.

Phyl ran up to him as he sat on the bench, unlacing his shoes.

"Hey, man, you did okay," she said.

He looked up at her. He suspected that a few guys nearby had heard her, and he blushed. "Thanks, Phyl."

She stood there a few seconds longer, then said, "Take care," and dashed away.

He watched her a bit, then turned back to finish unlacing his shoes.

"Hey, wasn't that Monahan?" he heard one of the guys say.

"Yeah, that was Monahan," another replied.

Eddie ignored them.

15

Eddie didn't see Phyllis during the next several days.
He thought about her a lot. He felt a strong desire to
give her a call, to ask her if she'd like to play catch
with him, or pepper, or go for a swim in the gulf, but
he fought the impulse. Was this what Harry meant
by falling for someone? Heck, he was just interested
in making sure that she could play again and not be
afraid of a pitched ball, he tried to tell himself.

He was sure she had conquered most of that goal.
The only thing he wasn't sure about was her batting
against him. Secretly he wished that she wouldn't
have to, but he checked the schedule and saw that
the Lancers were playing the Surfs on Tuesday.

He didn't know whether she was working out with
the Surfs or not. Most teams quit practicing toward
the latter part of the season. The Lancers hadn't
practiced the last two weeks. They were in third
position. Eddie suspected that maybe Coach Inger
might think the team couldn't possibly end up higher
than that, anyway.

Tip called him on the phone Monday evening.

"Hey," he said. "Did you read the sports pages in the *Argus Tribune*?"

He hadn't had a chance to. His father was reading it.

"No. Why?"

"Her picture's in it."

Eddie frowned. "Phyl's?"

"Yeah. With a nice article about her. She's playing tomorrow. We're playing the Surfs, you know."

"I know," said Eddie. He rubbed his forehead. "You think Mr. Inger will have me pitch against her, Tip?"

"I don't know. You worried about it?"

"Well — no."

That wasn't the whole truth. The whole truth was that he wasn't *too* worried. Heck, what were the odds of a pitcher hitting the same batter twice? And in the back of the head yet?

"I bet the picture and article about her will draw a big crowd," Tip said.

"I bet it will, too," Eddie agreed.

He'd been overwhelmingly happy once he was sure that she was healthy enough and fearless enough to compete again. But he visualized a biased crowd that might be attending only because of what they had read about Phyllis Monahan, the girl who played

on an all-boy baseball team, who had been incapaci-
tated because of a wild pitch thrown by a certain
Eddie Rhodes and who might face him again in her
first game since her injury.

He was afraid a small story might get blown out of
proportion just because of that picture and article.

But, if he felt that he'd be under pressure from the
fans if he were to pitch, what about her? Wouldn't
she be as sensitive about it as he?

"Well, I just wondered if you'd seen the paper,"
said Tip.

"Yeah. Okay. Thanks, Tip. Hey, wait a minute."

"What?"

"If you're not doing anything, bring over your
trumpet."

"I'm not doing anything," said Tip.

Eddie grinned. "Good. I'll see ya."

He hung up and sat there awhile, concentrating
his attention on a fly that was buzzing outside against
the window. But his mind was on the upcoming game
against the Surfs. Well, it should prove interesting,
he told himself.

Tip came over twenty minutes later, carrying the
worn case in which he kept his bright and shiny
trumpet. Mr. and Mrs. Rhodes had gone outside to
inspect their garden, so the boys took advantage of
their absence, and for half an hour they had a jam

session in the living room, Tip blowing the trumpet as loudly as he could, Eddie banging the snares and rattling the cymbals. For a while everything but the music was forgotten — even baseball.

The weather the next afternoon was hot and sunny, hotter and sunnier than Eddie liked. Because of the publicity the newspaper article had generated, Mr. Rhodes promised Eddie that come game time he'd be there in the stands. He wanted to see if this Monahan girl was really as good as the paper said she was.

He didn't say he also wanted to see how Eddie performed against her if he pitched. But Eddie suspected it.

Roxie and Margie promised to be there, too. The game would be over in plenty of time for Roxie to relieve their mother at the gift shop.

Eddie, Tip, and Puffy arrived at the park just as the other guys and Coach Inger did. Some of the Surfs were already there, taking batting practice. One of them was Phyl.

The Surfs' equipment was strewn in front of the third-base dugout, an indication that they were going to have last bats.

After Coach Inger dumped the Lancers' equipment in front of the first-base dugout, Tip lifted a baseball out of the canvas bag and started to play catch with Eddie and Puffy. Some of the other Lancers started playing catch, too. Some, pepper ball.

"She's batting," remarked Tip.

Eddie turned to look at her. She had on a helmet, and stood at the plate in a spread-eagle, fearless stance. The kid on the mound pitched one in and Phyl rapped it over shortstop.

"Tip, work out with Harry," Eddie heard Coach Inger say. "I'm going to have him start."

"Okay."

Tip smiled as he tossed the ball back to Eddie. "Relieved?" he asked.

He shrugged. He guessed he was.

He found himself listening to the sound of Phyl's bat connecting with the balls, and felt a secret thrill that she was pounding the ball so well. It proved to him that his helping her had worked. But practice pitches were no solid proof that she could hit as successfully in a game. The real test was how she performed after the ump called "play ball!"

In routine fashion the Lancers took batting practice after the Surfs finished theirs, then infield practice. When the Surfs had the field, Eddie watched Phyl from the bench, saw her scoop up grounders hit to her by her coach, and whip the ball to second, third, and home with remarkable ease.

He looked at the crowd. As he expected, the stands were filled almost to capacity.

They cheered and clapped as the Surfs went out on the field. Some of them yelled at Phyllis, letting her know that they were there to support her. She responded with a smile and a brief wave of her hand.

"Hey, Larry! Hey, Larry!" Dale piped up as the leadoff man stepped to the plate.

"Get the big one, Larry! Get the big one!" Tip yelled.

Don was coaching at first, clapping his hands, yelling, his cap brim pulled low to shield his eyes from the sun. Mr. Inger was coaching at third, pulling on his cap brim, spitting on his hands, rubbing them together.

Eddie looked at Phyl. She was leaning forward slightly, pounding a fist into her mitt, her voice joined in the chatter with her teammates. She was blending in well after being out of the game so long, he reflected.

A tall left-hander named Dick Fleming was pitching for the Surfs. He looked calm, relaxed. He stretched, kicked, delivered, and in short order disposed of Larry, Rod, and Dale.

131

Harry didn't do badly, either. One, two, three — he bowled over the Surfs' first three hitters.

Fleming's performance was repeated in the top of the second, but at their turn at bat Bob Adams, their center fielder, slashed out a single over Puffy's head and went to second base on a sacrifice bunt.

Phyllis came up, cheers and applause greeting her the minute she started for the batter's box.

"Talk about a celebrity," said Don, sitting next to Eddie.

"Yeah," Eddie murmured softly.

He felt a nervous twitching in his stomach. This was the part of the game he was waiting for. The part that counted for her. And for him.

She took a ball and a strike. Then she laid into one. The ball rocketed to deep center. It was high. It looked like a sure homer. Eddie got to his feet, his mouth clasped tightly, his breath held. The fans too had risen and were cheering madly.

The ball came down inside the park. Lynn reached high for it and caught it.

The roar of the crowd died. There was a sound of sadness in it. But the drive had advanced the runner to third, and then he scored on D. D. Davis's double.

Eddie sat down, his heart beating hard. It was close to being a home run, he thought. Very close.

Puffy started a hitting spree for the Lancers in the top of the third. His single, Larry's double, and Rod's triple combined to pile up three runs to put them ahead of the Surfs, 3 to 1.

In the fourth, Phyl rapped out a smashing single, but got thrown out at second on a double play. Her slide into the bag was just as neat as any ballplayer's Eddie had ever seen.

The score remained unchanged until the bottom of the fifth when the Surfs began spraying the baseball all over the lot.

"Eddie! Warm up!" Coach Inger told him.

The call startled Eddie. He'd been wrapped up in the game.

"Come on, Pete," he said.

He stepped out of the dugout, picked up one of the loose balls lying on the ground near the bat rack, and went down behind the first-base bleachers. Pete Turner followed him with a catcher's mitt.

He began throwing easily, feeling the kinks in his shoulders loosen until he could throw them in hard enough to make the ball sound like a rifle shot as it hit Pete's mitt.

He heard a familiar call and saw the coach waving him in. Harry was finished.

But he wasn't leaving the game. He was replacing Tony in right field.

Eddie tossed the practice ball to Pete and took his time walking out to the mound. A few cheers and casual remarks greeted him.

He got on the mound, tossed in a few practice throws, and was ready to go.

Examining the situation, he saw that runners were on first and second.

Tip trotted out to him, his shin guards, belly guard, and mask looking bulky on him.

"Great spot to put you in," he muttered quietly. "There are two on and only one out."

"How many runs they got?"

"Two." Tip's eyes glittered through the mask. "See who's second batter?"

Eddie glanced toward the Surfs' on-deck circle. Phyllis was bent there on one knee, grasping a bat.

"Yeah," he said.

Tip slapped him on the butt. "Let's get 'em."

Pierce, the Surfs' catcher, was up. So far he had laid down a sacrifice bunt and flied out. A hit now could score another run. Maybe two. Eddie realized his disadvantages.

He threw two low pitches, the second around Pierce's knees. Pierce bit at it and popped up. Two outs.

Phyl got off her knee and walked up to the plate. Her fans applauded her. A few added comments.

"There's your chance, Phyl! Drill it down his throat!"

"Blast it back at him, Phyl! On the head!"

"A home run! Pile it on, Phyl!"

Eddie stood behind the mound, collecting his wits. He avoided meeting her eyes, and concentrated on the sign that Tip was giving him, and then on Tip's target that looked like a big eye of a bull.

He threw two on the outside corner for balls. And then, for one moment, he met Phyl's eyes squarely. They were sharp and alert. Her lips were grim. There was only one thing clearly outlined in her piercing glance: she was determined to hit that ball.

He grooved one in for a called strike, and aimed the next one for the inside corner. For just one moment he thought that the ball had gotten away from him, that it was going to be another wild shot.

But it was just inside the plate, close enough to her to force her back a little.

Eddie breathed a sigh of relief. The crowd hissed.

"Tag it, Phyl!" a fan yelled.

Eddie grooved the next one, and she swung. Wood connected horsehide. The ball shot out to deep left center field, a rainbow arc halfway between Dale and Lynn, who began busting their tails after it.

The ball hit the fence and rolled back. Harry

retrieved it and pegged it in, holding Phyl up at third.

The crowd's yell was like thunder.

"You did it, Phyl! You did it!" a fan yelled loudly, and Eddie could see Mingo standing and clapping like crazy up in the grandstand behind the backstop screen.

The next batter flied out and the inning was over. Lancers 3, Surfs 5.

"Don't let it get you down," Tip said as Eddie came walking in.

"I'm not."

Puffy looked at him. "You figure you're even now?"

Eddie shrugged. "Even with what? She got a good solid hold of the ball. What's there to get even about?"

Puffy smiled, and socked him lightly on the arm.

"Right on, Eddie."

The Lancers picked up two runs, and the Surfs two.

In the top of the seventh, Larry, Rod, and Dale all went down under Fleming's smoke, and it was over. The Surfs took the game, 7–5.

Eddie walked off the field. He felt a mixture of dejection and satisfaction. He hated to have lost the game, but that was secondary to what he was thinking about Phyllis Monahan. She could play baseball again, and stand up to his pitching without fear. Nothing was more important than that.

He saw Coach Inger waiting for him with a smile. "Nice game, Eddie," he said, taking Eddie's hand. "You pitched a fine ball game."

"Thanks, Coach."

The Surfs came over and shook hands with the losers. Suddenly Eddie found himself face to face with Phyllis.

"Good game, Eddie," she said, her face shining with sweat.

He smiled. "Nice hit, Phyl. You've really come back. Just like a champ."

"Thanks to you."

For a moment she blinked, then she turned and ran off, her cap in her hand, her hair flying in the wind.

"Hey, Eddie!" Tip called to him. "You coming?"

He took off his cap and wiped his forehead.

"I'm coming," he said. "Hold your horses."